Destiny's Winding Road

Other Books by LaJoyce Martin:

The Harris Family Saga:
To Love a Bent-Winged Angel
Love's Mended Wings
Love's Golden Wings
When Love Filled the Gap
To Love a Runaway
A Single Worry
Two Scars Against One
The Fiddler's Song
The Artist's Quest

Pioneer Romance:
The Wooden Heart
Heart-Shaped Pieces
Light in the Evening Time
To Strike a Match
Love's Velvet Chains
Destiny's Winding Road

Historical Romance:
So Swift the Storm
So Long the Night

Historical Novel:
Thread's End

Western:
The Other Side of Jordan
To Even the Score

Path of Promise:
The Broken Bow
Ordered Steps

Children's Short Stories:
Batteries for My Flashlight

Nonfiction:
Mother Eve's Garden Club
Heroes, Sheroes, and a Few Zeroes
I'm Coming Apart, Lord!

Order from:
Pentecostal Publishing House
8855 Dunn Road
Hazelwood, MO 63042-2299

Destiny's Winding Road

by LaJoyce Martin

Destiny's Winding Road

by LaJoyce Martin

©1998 Word Aflame Press
Hazelwood, MO 63042-2299

Cover Design by Paul Povolni
Cover Art by Bob Watkins

All Scripture quotations in this book are from the King James Version of the Bible unless otherwise identified.

Printed in United States of America.

Printed by

Library of Congress Cataloging-in-Publication Data

Martin, LaJoyce, 1937–
    Destiny's winding road / by LaJoyce Martin.
        p. cm.
    ISBN 1-56722-211-0
    I. Title.
PS3563.A72486D47   1998
813'.54—dc21
                                   97-49671
                                    CIP

To
The Littlest Angel,
Ashton Jade

Contents

THE STORY

"Take her! Oh, please take her!"

A dying mother's plea, clothed in desperation, reached Dorchan's ears above the holocaust. Then with her last surge of strength, the woman flung an infant from the upper balcony of a burning building and disappeared into the flames.

Dorchan caught the falling bundle. The hand-crafted quilt that cosseted the child seemed more substantial than its contents, but Dorchan hadn't time for rational thought. Her life—and now the life of the quilt-clad baby—depended on her expeditious escape down Wabash Avenue, a street packed with hundreds of pedestrians fleeing the fire. Would any of them make it to safety?

"Hurry! Hurry!" A ruddy-faced policeman urged them on. From an offshore railroad trestle, a locomotive whistled its final note. "The death knell!" yelled a berserk runner, shoving through the horde.

"How could such a fate befall us on the Lord's Day?" a woman near Dorchan cried.

"I'd call this the Devil's Day, madam," a jeering voice countered.

"Methinks it's the Judgment Day," put in another.

The distance between Michigan Avenue and the lake,

almost a mile, was littered with abandoned items that the rousted residents had tried to salvage from their homes and then cast aside, revealing reason and panic in close juxtaposition. Actions and reactions fostered a contrast of hysterical laughter and bitter weeping. Curses intermingled with prayers.

A small, barefoot girl limped down the street, crooning to four puppies in a box. She was overtaken by a man brandishing a feather duster.

"Pardon me, please." A stout, florid woman excused her way through the throng, bumping a bulky trunk behind her. "My husband's urn of ashes is in here. No one should get ashed twice."

The crowd snaked and turned, causing Dorchan to lose her bearing. With flames on three sides of them, only a narrow passageway remained clear. Then for one awful moment, the fire closed the exit ahead with its crimson wall. Hope died in Dorchan's heart. They were doomed!

We shall be turned to cinders, she told herself, grieving more for the child than for herself. Whoever the infant might be, she hadn't had a chance at life. Her beginning and ending chapters left no room for a biography between.

But the wind shifted, leaving the street open again. The hodgepodge of humanity tramped on doggedly, passing the imminent danger, and when they had reached the Northern Section, a clergyman waved Dorchan into a great stone church. Wearily, she dropped into a pew, glad for the hush that provided a respite from the bedlam outside. It seemed that she had been on her feet fleeing the death angel forever.

Her burden was quiet and still. *Too still.* A new horror accosted Dorchan. *The baby was dead!* It was a corpse when its mother let it fall, or else it had been killed by the plunge. Dorchan ripped back the covering, and two small eyes peered up at her. "You are alive," she breathed, relief bringing tears.

Dorchan allowed that she must have dozed, for she was jolted to awareness by frantic voices. "The brewery has caught! Head for the lake!" As a single unit, the congregation scrambled toward a barren stretch of beach called the Sands.

Here the baby set up a pitiful howl of hunger, and Dorchan prevailed upon a nursing mother to share her own baby's portion of breast milk with the nameless infant. The baby had a sweet, milky odor when she was passed back to Dorchan.

Darkness clamped down upon the shore dwellers, and a miserable night it was. Before sunrise, a woman near Dorchan fell dead. No one knew who she was.

The smells: burning feather mattresses, baked fur, scorched hair, . . . Dorchan's empty stomach heaved and protested. She splashed water from the lake onto her face to quell her illness.

As day broke that Monday morning, a stranger offered Dorchan a crust of hard bread, and she took it. "Thank you," she murmured. "You are indeed generous."

"You must survive, little mother," the benefactor smiled. "A child's destiny rests upon you."

Dorchan began to move with the throng on land as they inched up the north shore. At the first opportunity, she took shelter in a wooden shack occupied by other mothers and children. She supposed her filled arms would qualify her as a mother, at least a temporary one.

11

As more and more shelter-seekers crowded into the unstable building, the floor suddenly sagged, and the walls started giving way. Sensing the peril, Dorchan fled just before the shed collapsed. Would she never find a haven?

Footsore, discouraged, and more tired than she had ever been, Dorchan finally found refuge at a farmhouse with twenty others.

On Monday evening, October 9, 1871, the rain came—a glorious drizzle that ended the Great Chicago Fire, which had destroyed 73 miles of streets, 17,500 buildings, and an unknown score of people. Dorchan was numbered among the 100,000 left homeless.

Dorchan's story begins in 1874, three years after the fire that made her the sole guardian of a baby she did not ask for, could not refuse and would not give up. It is a drama all its own.

ONE

GAME'S END

"Mommy, when is our daddy coming?"

Dorchan stared out the window. Early that morning, a light snow powdered the ground. Viewed from above, it might appear that God had spread a thin layer of white icing on a huge, marbled sheet cake and that a naughty child poked his fingers in the frosting, leaving holes here and there.

Now the sun had come out to lick away the rest of the topping. But the same warm influence did nothing to thaw Dorchan's heart. Although her eyes could still see and her ears could still hear, her world had gone dead. It seemed that a spring had broken inside her, and the whole clock of life had stopped.

Her wedding dress hung on a wall peg, mocking her. She had waited three years for Paul Wickerton to take her to the altar, and last week she'd learned that Paul planned to wed someone else. How could she explain the betrayal to Destiny?

"Daddy Paul isn't coming, Destiny. He has found another mommy."

"And a little girl?"

"No."

"He doesn't *want* us?" The question bit hard.

Children could be brutally frank, going to the inflamed core of a matter.

For days they had played a game called "When Daddy gets here, we will . . . ," with each shouting imaginary activities. Destiny's ideas were fishing, riding a pony, or playing hide-and-seek. Dorchan's suggestions included reading stories, snuggling on the horsehair sofa, and eating popcorn together.

Now the game had ended. It ended because it was nothing more than that to Paul Wickerton—a game—and Dorchan the chess piece that was eliminated.

She pulled the child onto her lap, craving the warmth of the small body to counterbalance her own inner coldness. Rocking back and forth as a matter of habit, Dorchan lulled the little girl to sleep while chronicling the happenings since the fire had heaped instant motherhood upon her.

After hours of fleeing flames, she had found shelter at a farmhouse. She was a mere nineteen then, too young to be a woman and too old to be a child. She still remembered lying on a pallet, opening and closing her eyes, moving her legs beneath the ragged quilt. She was alive and surprised to be so.

Mary Wickerton, a woman who had mustered enough birthdays to be Dorchan's own mother, had cared for the baby, satiating the child's hunger with tepid goat's milk. Dorchan had no idea what she would have done without Mary, a capable and dauntless caretaker. When Dorchan told Mary the story of the child, Mary said, "Don't worry. We will find a good home for her."

"No, I will keep her," Dorchan replied. Her chin jutted. "God put her into my life for a reason. Some destiny was at work, and so I am naming her Destiny. She will fill an emptiness." Her voice cracked as it struggled to expel the last word.

"Oh, but my dear girl, you are so young!" objected Mary. "Do you realize the awesome responsibility of rearing a child? Besides food, clothing and shelter, there is education and—"

"God will help me."

"God helps those who help themselves. You would not be wise to yoke yourself with such a burden! Someday you will wish to marry and have children of your own. We will find a *very* good family for Destiny."

"No!" Dorchan's set jaw brooked no argument.

"If you insist . . ."

"I insist."

"And after losing your entire family in the fire—"

"I had no family. I know nothing of my background. I was reared in an orphanage until I was fifteen years old, at which time I hired out as a live-in servant. The lady for whom I worked was downtown when the South Section caught. I can only assume she is among the fatalities. I escaped with the clothing on my back and my handbag, but I had little else to mourn. This baby gives me a purpose to live. An orphan myself, I will understand her struggles."

"The orphanage could shed no light on your origin, dear?" Mary was nosy, but she meant well.

"The matron said that I was deposited at the institution when I was approximately a year old by a man who said he was my father and that he would return for me. He hurried away and never came back. Along with me, he left a purse and a parasol. In the purse were a few coins and a picture of me with the inscription on the back: *Dorchan at six months.*"

"No surname?"

"The man left no name, no address. They called me Brown because of my brown cape."

"How ironic! Neither you nor the baby will ever know who you are or your birth dates."

"That's why I think that more than mere happenstance brought us together," Dorchan beamed. "We are two of a kind, alone in the world, destined to help each other. All life has a pattern designed by the Master Weaver."

"How will you support the child?"

"I don't know yet, but I'll manage. I am no stranger to hard work or poor fare. She will be better off with me than in the poorhouse. I speak from experience; I have been there."

In retrospect, how Dorchan came to stay on with Mary Wickerton was unclear. Mary was a large-hearted lady but controlling. She arranged Dorchan's life for her week by week, decision by decision.

It didn't seem a bad arrangement; Mary's domination scotched Dorchan's insecurity. They got along well. The householder was a woman of extreme thrift. She patched the torn places and then patched the patches in rent fabric and in Dorchan's raveled life.

Right away Mary recognized in the younger woman an extraordinary talent for sewing. Accustomed to milking from everything its amplitude, she stationed Dorchan at the machine for long hours. It took skill to guide the cloth with one hand and turn the machine's wheel with the other, but Dorchan learned fast. After a short period of

16

tutoring, Mary had her making garments of rare elegance. Within a few weeks, Dorchan was stitching gowns for three top-drawer boutiques, as well as designing hats for a millinery shop. With scraps of material from these jobs, she made adorable dresses for Destiny. It was a perk of the work that she liked best.

Mary Wickerton delivered the wares and brought Dorchan her wage, out of which she kept a portion for Dorchan's room and board. In the meantime, Mary became attached to the child, proclaiming Destiny the most beautiful and best dressed youngster in Cook County. And, indeed, Destiny—with a thousand golden ringlets—was a delightful child, eye pleasing and easy tempered.

Dorchan hadn't been with Mary long when Mary mentioned her son, Paul, enrolled in a faraway academy. Most of Mary's money, Dorchan learned, went to the young man. Luxuries were forbidden so that Paul might have a proper education.

Subtly and with a mother's prejudice, Mary painted Paul's picture with broad and colorful strokes. On the canvas of her mind, Paul was the perfect mate for Dorchan. He was handsome and brilliant. And he would certainly be ready for marriage when he completed his schooling, Mary said. She fed Dorchan on a menu of her son's finest attributes until Dorchan built a world of dreams on the bias of Mary's verbal yardage.

On Paul's infrequent visits to his mother's home, Dorchan savored every crumb of attention he paid her. While Mary kept Destiny, they walked in the woods, watched sunsets, and went to town for sodas together. Paul paid Destiny scant attention, but Dorchan excused his actions. In fact, she excused a host of his taciturn moods. When they were married, Paul would bond with Destiny.

The child stirred in Destiny's arms, bringing her back to the present. "Mommy, who will play horsey with me?"

"Go back to sleep, darling. We'll talk about it later."

Mary had encouraged Dorchan to have patience with Paul, her only offspring. She was sure that he loved Dorchan and Destiny; he just wasn't an overly affectionate boy. "He tells me that he plans to get married when his education is complete," Mary repeated.

Dorchan ignored the scratches at the door of reality. She should have noticed that Paul came home dressed to the nines while his mother wore a ragged chemise. Why didn't she divine that Paul's good disposition ran in direct symmetry with the amount of money he was able to siphon from his mother? Men were an enigma to Dorchan, incomprehensible and vague.

She and Mary had a marvelous time fashioning the wedding dress; Mary had even allowed an extra dollar for pearl buttons. When they were finished, they pulled down the calendar and counted the days until Paul would come for his bride. Five more months. Then four. Then three. . . .

Then came the last holiday before graduation: the Easter break, 1874. Paul would surely be more attentive, knowing that he could soon give his full homage to a family and a future.

Dorchan's hopes burgeoned. Spring vacation! Green shoots pushing through the damp, pungent earth. Streams burbling. Birds building nests. The wind ruffling her hair. And Paul coming home. . . .

However, Dorchan sensed a difference in Paul when he walked through the door. A restlessness. A distraction of mind. She made allowances for him again; he was weary from the intense study for his final examinations. The old bantering they had enjoyed in the past was missing, the camaraderie gone. When Destiny leaned on his knee, he roughly shooed her away.

So disturbed was Dorchan's spirit that she took Destiny's hand and walked outside. The wind had changed to the north and turned nippy, and Destiny needed a coat. Not wanting to go back through the sitting room where Paul and his mother conversed, Dorchan climbed in the low window to her room to get the wrap. Inside, she could hear Mary's voice quite clearly. Something premonitory stopped her as still as a corpse.

Mary was agitated. "For all these months, I thought you cared for Dorchan, and now—"

"Shh, Mother. She will hear you."

"She isn't here. I saw her and Destiny walking toward the pasture."

"Then what better time to tell you? My life is my own, and—"

"You will never find anyone as precious as Dorchan, Paul. She can sew. She can cook. She is a real Christian. And she's patient. If you want to take some time to see the world, she will wait."

"Please stop talking long enough to listen. I'm trying to tell you something. I don't want to see the world. I am engaged to be married. To *someone else!*"

"Paul—no!"

"Mother, yes! I was never in love with Dorchan."

"But I thought—"

19

"You thought! You thought! Well, think again. I love Aurilla."

"It isn't possible, Paul."

"It is possible, and it is true. You've let your sympathy get the better of you. You know nothing at all of Dorchan's background. All you have is her story, which may or may not be true. Have you considered that Destiny could well be Dorchan's own child?"

"Dorchan is honest."

"Dorchan! Dorchan! Dorchan is honest. Dorchan is pretty. Dorchan is sweet. I'm sick of hearing about Dorchan! You've always tried to control my life, but this time you shall not. I'm marrying a woman with money. Dorchan is as poor as a church mouse. The girl to whom I am espoused has education, an inheritance, and refinement."

"But what about Dorchan? She has her wedding dress made—"

"Her wedding dress? I made no commitment to her! I'm sorry if she misunderstood my brotherly consideration."

"But I was so sure you would want her for your wife."

"Well, I don't. I want neither a ready-made family nor a woman with questionable morals."

"Paul, please—"

"I hope that you can accept Aurilla and be proud of her, for if you don't you will lose both of us."

"Of course, son, I will . . . I will try to accept her. But how will she react to Dorchan?"

"I'm afraid it will be uncomfortable for Dorchan when I bring Aurilla home. Perhaps it would be best for all concerned if Dorchan would find another place to live."

"I can't just turn her out. There's little Destiny—"

"Take your choice, Mother. I am your son, your flesh and blood. Surely Dorchan can make enough with her sewing to rent a room elsewhere. She has mooched off you long enough. I insist that you ask her to move."

Dorchan bit her lip to hold back a wild cry. The man on whom she had pinned her dreams had just dismissed her from his future and had thrown a shadow on her pure character. Her hand fluttered to her throat. Like a tree cut deeply into its trunk, she felt herself begin to weaken, toppling toward despair. Standing numbly, knowing her hopes had fled, she wondered if there was some way to ready herself for the blade of disappointment's guillotine.

"What's wrong, Mommy?"

"Let's play the quiet game, Destiny," she had whispered. "Crawl back out the window, and let's race to the road." She needed to get away quickly to think.

Mary Wickerton must never know that she had overheard. She would spare the woman the pain of evicting her. Where she would go or what she would do she did not know, but God would show her. *Won't You, God?*

Slipping through the orchard, she took the road that led to the log church where she worshiped with a small congregation each Lord's Day. "Is it church day?" Destiny asked, looking down at her clothes. "My pretty dress isn't put on yet."

"It isn't church day, but I need to talk to God," explained Dorchan.

"Will He be there today?"

"I hope so."

The empty church furnished no consolation. Dorchan's prayers echoed back to her from the rafters, deadlocked in the deserted building. She had gotten no answers, found no solutions that day. She'd faced a bleak watershed of her life, her emotions flowing one way and her reason another. Had it not been for Destiny, she would have struck out afoot, not returning to Mary Wickerton's for her clothes, her savings, or a farewell. She didn't want to see Paul Wickerton now or ever.

The next few hours forced upon Dorchan the bitter certainty that she was no longer wanted. She and her child were nomads in a hostile wilderness. Would she, like the dove Noah sent from the window of the ark, wander to and fro, finding no rest for the sole of her foot?

She told Mary that she didn't feel well, which wasn't untruth. Boycotting the family meals, she slipped into the kitchen for leftovers to feed Destiny. She ate little herself, her appetite gone.

She gave thanks that Paul didn't stay long. He was anxious to get back to the life he had built for himself. Before he left, he wheedled more money from his mother, promising repayment later.

After Paul's departure, Mary wept often, suffering bouts of depression. Sick headaches beset her. Perhaps she thought that Paul would reconsider and change his plans. Or perhaps she hadn't the nerve to tell Dorchan the truth. For whatever reason, she didn't mention her son's forthcoming wedding. She just said that Paul had a problem that begged prayer. . . .

Here the past joined the present as the end of Destiny's nap brought the curtain down on Dorchan's flashback. "Huh, Mommy? Who will play with me?"

"I will play with you, dearest. You and I will move far, far away."

"But I want a daddy. Daddies are big and strong, and they go to work so mommies can stay home with Destinys. And if we move far, far away, what will Granny Mary do? She will cry."

Dorchan didn't want to answer questions; she didn't want to think or plan or remember.

"And you won't wear the pretty white dress?" asked the child.

"No." The word was flat, bitter tasting.

Dorchan had waited a very long time for her dream to come true, but the nightmare had come quickly and without mercy. The hurt sank deeply inside her into the center of her soul, ricocheting to the pit of her stomach.

That night, her pillow sponged up the tears.

TWO

THE SEARCH

Dorchan felt the pinch of time. She must find a place to go. And soon. There had been no voices from heaven, no writing in the clouds. Surely, she thought, God must be sleeping, unaware of her predicament.

When she announced to Mary Wickerton that she was leaving, Mary tried with little success to hide her relief. "I will miss you, Dorchan," the troubled woman said, "and I will grieve for Destiny. But I know that you cannot always depend upon others for emotional support. The time has come for you to make your own life. I had hoped that you would marry my son, but I have come to realize that the two of you are not suited to each other. You have nothing in common. Your worlds revolve in different orbits. I am not sure that it would even be wise for you and me to keep in contact over the years. It might cause pain for both of us."

"I will not bother you, Mary."

Dorchan was not without funds, thankfully. She had diligently saved her wages each week, accumulating more than a hundred dollars. That amount would buy luggage and take her anywhere in the United States, the farther from Chicago and its bitter memories the better.

With each passing day, she felt Mary's not-so-subtle

nudges embodied in such remarks as, "Is there anything I can do to help you pack, dear?"

Dorchan always answered her kindly, her face aching with the pleasant expression that was fixed there, "Thank you, Mary, but everything is right on schedule." Was the declaration faith or wishful thinking?

Go south. One morning during prayer, distinct direction came of its own accord. From whence the impression sprang, Dorchan didn't know, nor did she question. She had to go some direction, and south was as good as any.

With this inner goading, she needed but an hour to prepare for her departure. She coiled her abundant hair into a chignon, anchored it with a crimping pin, and gathered her trunks.

Mary took them to the train station to see them off, not bothering to inquire after Dorchan's destination. It was unlike Mary not to ask questions, and her lack of concern smarted. But Dorchan was glad Mary didn't pry, for in truth she had no destination. She supposed she simply would ride south until she felt an urge to get off. Then she would rent a room and look for work.

Caught up in the childish ecstasy of riding a "really real train," Destiny coped with the parting well. Dorchan was grateful for this small miracle. Tears would have been the last straw on her overtaxed constitution; she was too near the breaking point herself. Adrift in the world, she had never been attacked more by desolation.

Once on the transport and moving, Dorchan took inventory. She had three large trunks, money to suffice for several weeks, and a healthy child. On the minus side, she had a broken heart, a useless wedding dress, and no family for support. Things could be better, but then again, they could be worse. She and Destiny could be crippled and scarred from burns. She supposed that the raw places in her mind would eventually heal over, and new faith would grow through the cracks of the crushing disillusion. At least, she hoped so.

She had been such a fool to think that Paul Wickerton loved her! She blushed at her naiveté. It was all her fault, this bruise of thwarted expectation. He had given her no vocalized cause to believe he cared for her, but given her lack of romantic experience and Mary's match-making efforts, she had no definition by which to judge his "brotherly" actions. She had judged them wrongly.

Destiny laid her head on Dorchan's lap, letting the click of the wheels lull her to sleep. Dorchan closed her eyes, too, willing the mental fog to burn off and allowing a sudden, drowsy peace to swallow her. Tomorrow would be time enough to deliberate on the future.

Daylight had forsaken the coach when she roused. *Where was she?* Oh, yes, the train . . . *South* . . . A porter stood beside her, holding a sack in his hand. "Ma'am, you and the child slept clean through dinner. I saw how exhausted you were, so I didn't bother you. Knowing you would be hungry, though, I wrapped you some ham and biscuit in a napkin here." He pushed his offering toward her. "The sleeping berth is ready when you are."

Dorchan smiled her gratitude. "Thank you, sir. I am very tired."

She lifted Destiny into her arms and moved to the sleeper. The food went untouched; both she and the child slept through the night as the locomotive crept up mountains, sledded down valleys, sped past slumbering villages, and stopped at city depots. Where the conveyance was taking her, Dorchan neither knew nor cared.

Dawn brought an unfamiliar topography. The world through which they now passed seemed to be constructed on a larger scale than the one they'd left behind. The terrain heaved with mounds, timber-topped hills, and grassy basins drenched in spring colors, wild and untamed. It was virgin land, scattershot with a neighborless cottage here and there. How would she know when she had reached the "right" place? This couldn't be it, of course. Besides the lack of habitation, it wasn't far enough removed from her past.

When Destiny awoke, she was a bundle of questions: Where are we? When will we be home? Where is Granny Mary? Will she visit us in our new home? Do trains have cookies or crackers or jelly? Answering in monosyllables, Dorchan steered Destiny toward the dining car.

She buttered the child's oatmeal, but her own desire for food flagged. In its place was an indescribable pain, a longing for family or a friend. Who would know or care when her journey ended or where? Mary wanted to be rid of her so that she might embrace Paul's bride. *Should I die*, Dorchan concluded, *there would be no mourners. I wouldn't even be missed.* A distressing summary but true. *If only I had one friend . . .*

A chirpy voice brought Dorchan's mind scrambling back from her cave of melancholy. "My! What a brown study! Life can't be *that* bad. May I join you?" Insouciant eyes waited until Dorchan, managing a begrudging smile, nodded.

"Oh, that's better." The speaker, a girl about Dorchan's age, wore too much rouge, heavy eye paint, and a dress with a neckline that revealed more than it should. "Boy, it's nice to find a friend! My name is Roxie; what's yours?"

"Dorchan."

"Dorchan. Hmm. Now that's an unusual name. Do you like it?"

"Yes."

She made a wry face. "I hate my name. I don't know why I couldn't have been named Diana or Athena or one of the other beautiful goddesses." She stopped and focused her gaze on Destiny. "Stuck with your baby sister, eh?"

"She's my daughter. That is—"

"*Daughter?* Is your husband with you?" She made a quick survey of the car and prattled on. "That messes up everything. Who can have a good time with a demanding husband?"

"I have no husband."

"He's dead?"

"I've never been married."

"Oh." She raised her brows, but Dorchan failed to interpret the gesture for what it meant. "How interesting. And what is your prow and aft?"

"My what?"

"Where are you headed, and what's behind you?"

"I came from Chicago yesterday."

"And your landing?"

"I'm not—sure."

"Just joy riding, are you?"

"I'm going south to look for work."

"A job might be hard to come by with a youngster."

"I have a ready hand for sewing."

"Sewing?"

"I made dresses for a reputable shop in Chicago. I have a letter of recommendation with me."

"There's no money in sewing." Roxie pursed her red lips into a bow. "Besides, it's too much work. There's better ways for a single girl to earn money. I make twenty dollars a day."

"Twenty dollars a *day*?"

"I have made as high as fifty."

"In one day?"

"In one day."

"I'd like a job like that."

"I can always use a sidekick. If you want to hitch up with me, we can split expenses and make a boodle. We could hire someone to nurse your kid."

It sounded like a great solution, having a partner to share the cost of rent and food. Could this be Dorchan's answer? Roxie didn't look like a girl of character, but behind the mask of garish makeup might be a virtuous, caring comrade. One of Mary's favorite axioms was "You can't tell a book by its cover."

The wages Roxie mentioned were unbelievable. Dorchan had never known a man to command such exorbitant pay. Could the girl be teasing? She had rattled off the windfall with a straight face. "Are you on your way to such a position?" Dorchan asked, wanting more information.

"More or less. I'm headed for Abilene. We'll have to change trains in Kansas City and go west. Abilene isn't much of a town, I'm told, but that's where the cowboys from down in Oklahoma and Texas bring their cattle for sale. They say Abilene's streets are paved with gold for cowmen. And that means plenty of business."

"Business?"

"There's lot of saloons, and that opens opportunities for dance hall girls."

"What does that have to do with us?"

"Plenty. Can you dance?"

"N-no."

"Can you sing?"

"I sang once at Mrs. Wickerton's church."

Roxie lowered her voice. "Honey, I'm not talking about hallelujah stuff."

"Then I . . . I don't understand."

"You *are* green, aren't you? I'm talking about entertaining cowpokes the way they want to be entertained. *Any* way they want to be cajoled. That's where the money runs in rivers."

Dorchan whitened. "You're not talking about working as a street girl?"

Roxie laughed, a coarse, grating guffaw. "Exactly. But you learn little tricks early on, precious. If you don't want to defile your virtue, simply collect your wages first. Then get your customer so dead drunk that he doesn't know when he passes out. Just take your loot and leave."

Dorchan thought she might lose the few bites of toast that she had eaten. If she starved to death, she would never lower herself to such degradation. It was unthinkable!

"I won't be joining you, Roxie," Dorchan said, lifting clear eyes. "I had a mother, and although I do not remember her, something tells me that she was a pure and righteous Christian. I would bring shame to her memory if I should sully my reputation."

"Seems to me, dear, that your reputation is already

sullied," scoffed Roxie, "with a fatherless child." She pushed back her chair and sashayed from the dining car before Dorchan could offer explanation or reason.

THREE

A FRIEND

Elizabeth Brinnegar boarded the train at the St. Louis station. She had been to see her son who worked in the city, and as always, the parting saddened her. A hard lump sat in her throat.

On this visit, she had discerned that Howard's fellowship with God had been dulled and that new interests had crowded out his deep love for the Savior who had bought him. His once well-watered life was daily becoming more arid.

For two years, she had made the pilgrimage to Missouri in an effort to persuade Howard to come home. She needed him, and he needed her. But her pleading was wasted.

Elizabeth made her way to the chair car and took a seat, reflecting on the past week. Physically, Howard hadn't changed a lot. He had lost a bit of weight, yes, but it hadn't affected his statuesque handsomeness. The difference was in his eyes. They were haunted with a deep brooding, possessed of the hopeless solemnity of leaden skies. Whatever his argument, Elizabeth still felt that he would be better off—and less lonely—at home with her.

Turning her problems over in her mind, she took a seat near a young lady with a child. Her motherly eyes,

alert for ill-concealed hurts that constitute a life, fell on
Dorchan, whose honey-bronze hair had been plaited in a
thick braid to crown her head. This girl, Elizabeth decided, had seen more than her share of sorrows. She was
drawn to the little mother but especially to the lovely
child.

Elizabeth grinned at the little girl, prompting the
youngster to edge her way cautiously across the aisle.
"Hi!" the child said. "Do you know my Granny Mary?"

"Your Granny Mary? No, dear, but I'm sure she is a
lovely grandmother, and I should like very much to meet
her. She certainly is blessed to have such a lovely grandchild."

"Do you have a little girl?"

"No, but I wish I did. I have only one son, and he isn't
married."

Elizabeth looked up in time to see Dorchan's hands
twist and red coloring splash over her ears.

"You mustn't bother the nice lady, Destiny," admon-
ished Dorchan.

"Oh, she isn't bothering me!" Elizabeth assured. "I
love children."

"Daddy Paul found another mommy, and we still have
the pretty white dress," offered the innocent child. Then
with the caprice of the very young, she changed the subject abruptly. "What is your name?"

"Brinnegar. Elizabeth Brinnegar. And your name is—?"

"Destiny."

"What a pretty name!"

"My mother gave it to me."

"And this is your mother with you?"

"Uh-huh."

"Yes, ma'am," corrected Dorchan.

"Yes, ma'am, and my mother's name is Dorchan."

Elizabeth chortled. "And where do you live, Destiny?"

The child turned her small palms upward and hunched her shoulders. "Nowhere."

What had this young woman suffered? Heartbreak? Betrayal? Abandonment? Her tired, winsome face testified that she had not slept well for many nights. Elizabeth stanched a sudden impulse to take Dorchan into her arms, to shield her from whatever grief had stalked her. Without probing, she must find out how she could help.

Elizabeth moved to take a seat near Dorchan. "I know that you are suffering, my dear," she said, employing tact. "I am not trying to make your business mine, but if I may do anything to help you, I will be glad to do so. Do you need funds?"

"No," Dorchan answered. "I have enough money to take care of our present needs. But I thank you."

"You are going to relatives? Your mother, perhaps?"

"I have no mother. I was reared in an orphanage in Chicago. And I must explain that Destiny is not my child by birth, but she is just as dear to me. Destiny's mother asked that I take her child just before she died. I was to be married, or so I thought, to the man of whom Destiny spoke, one Paul Wickerton. But he chose another bride."

"And who is the grandmother the little one spoke about?"

"Mary wasn't any kin to us. She was Paul's mother. We lived with her for three years, and I worked as a seamstress. Since Paul has chosen to marry someone else, we had to leave. Destiny misses Mary very much."

"Of course. And I dare say Mary misses Destiny even more."

Dorchan said nothing.

"So where are you going, dear?"

Dorchan's fingers picked at a thread on her skirt. "I . . . I don't know."

"You have no destination?"

"Not yet. I'm praying . . ." Elizabeth saw that tears rode near the surface of Dorchan's eyes.

"Would you like to come home with me to stay until you find some direction for your future? I am a widow with a big house and a fenced yard that craves children—"

"Really, I must make my own way. It was so hard for Destiny to leave Mary that I cannot put her through another traumatic separation."

"I understand, but I believe God planned our meeting. The walls of my humble home have heard many prayers, and I would be pleased for you to consider it your lodging until you can find a place to your liking. And don't worry about the child fretting me. She will be a joy."

"Where do you live?"

"In central Texas, where the bluebonnets grow. The place is called Salado, and it is on the Lampasas River. It's just a speck of a town, but there is a nice stagecoach stop there. You can get transportation any direction from the inn."

"I could pay you—"

"I wouldn't think of letting you pay to be my honored guest."

"Please allow me to pray about it, Mrs. Brinnegar."

Roxie slipped from the car. She had been flirting with the porter, bustling from engine to caboose, tittering and

36

talking to male passengers, but she had heard Elizabeth's and Dorchan's conversation in its entirety. Her scornful glance suggested that she thought Dorchan had pulled a good one on the older lady in a ploy for sympathy. Her smirk said she could have made up a better story than that.

In her berth, Elizabeth sent up her own volley of petitions. From the looks of the girl, Dorchan couldn't be much past twenty, and life had already trounced her with a challenge and a battered heart. About abused hearts, Elizabeth knew. About challenges, she was still learning, and she would savor the enterprise of nurturing this unfinished woman, a child rearing a child. The mother inside her meshed into a pang of desire to love them both.

Dorchan, in her private sleeper, realized a more peaceful night than usual; she fell asleep praying, with Destiny on her right arm.

When Dorchan awoke, Elizabeth's offer still piqued her mind. Something in her spirit balked at the proposal. She didn't wish to become dependent upon or attached to another woman as she had Mary Wickerton. Furthermore, she had heard Elizabeth refer to an unmarried son. She wanted no more motherly matchmaking; she'd had enough of that.

Getting to Texas would take two or three more days or longer, depending on delays. At first, time had passed quickly. Now it hit patches of monotonous drag like a sled on melting ice. She was tired of traveling, tired of the swaying train. So ready was she for her journey to end that she would be pleased to get off at the next station.

Yet hadn't she prayed for God to give her direction, and hadn't Elizabeth come into her life almost immediately thereafter? What if God had sent the woman as an answer to her prayer and she failed to avail herself of His provisions? Then she would be on her own, a frightening prospect.

Destiny stirred, rubbing sleep from her eyes.

"Would you like to go visit the nice lady who talked with you yesterday?" Dorchan asked.

"Oh, yes, Mommy! May we? She told me about her flowers with their Sunday bonnets all in blue! It would be delicious to see them. She has a catty-kit, too. Could she be my Granny Elizabeth?"

"No more grannies, Destiny. Just friends."

"But grannies are gooder than friends. Grannies play games and tell stories and rock little girls."

After breakfast, Elizabeth pulled a peppermint stick from her purse for Destiny. "What do you say, Destiny?" prompted Dorchan.

"Thank you, and Mommy said that we might visit you and see the flowers with bonnets and your catty-kit, but I may not call you Granny. We will be just friends."

"With children there are no secrets." Dorchan's short laugh scarcely rose above the pain in her heart.

"Then you have decided to come home with me?" Elizabeth's voice was eager.

"Only for a short while. I must go somewhere to get settled so that I may make a living. Are there job opportunities in Texas?"

"Oh, many! We have been a state for nearly forty years, and we are popping buttons, so to speak. Have you any idea what you would like to do?"

"I wouldn't be particular as long as it was honest work. I can cook and clean and sew."

"Mr. Randleman hires a lot of people at the inn. He keeps a *Help Wanted* sign in the window most of the time. It is a nice, clean establishment with tolerable pay. Housing is furnished, I believe. Of course, you could live with me and walk or ride—"

"I wouldn't want to be a liability to anyone."

FOUR

THE PARTY

When Howard Brinnegar's mother boarded the Texas-bound train in St. Louis, he drew a long, deep breath and let it out slowly. He was glad that she was gone, glad that he had managed to keep her from finding out about Kona. He had been afraid that Elizabeth would not leave before the date of the party.

Elizabeth wouldn't approve of the upcoming bash where liquor would run freely and the music would incite hidden passions within one's soul. Nor would she approve of Kona, his boss's daughter. To climb the ladder of success, though, such gatherings (and bosses' daughters) could be useful affairs.

Howard had been apprehensive lest God reveal his secret to his mother. It had happened before, but this time it seemed that God didn't bother. Howard didn't know if that was good or bad, but it was a relief. Kona was not a Christian by any stretch of the word.

This was Howard's first party on Mr. Wantu's Mississippi River boat, and he planned to have a good time. Inch by inch he had been able to silence his conscience, break down the old-fashioned rules of his early training. When guilt reared its head, he struck at it with bitterness.

Howard's whole motive was to forget his past. That had been his purpose in coming to the city. No place on earth offered such seclusion as a large city. In small towns, everybody knew one's private life and felt free to question and discuss at will. But in a greater population, he could escape notice.

He frowned into the beveled mirror, struggling with his tie. Carefully, he smoothed his new shirt, examining each starched tuck, each seam, each buttonhole. Determination stared back at him from the looking glass, a mask with a thousand guises to hide a tortured soul. His was a handsome reflection, well proportioned to a six-foot frame, but he nonetheless loathed the image. Good looks didn't bring happiness.

This bitter young man once had been hurt by a woman. She had left him butchered and bleeding inside, and he had courted no one since. However, for this party he had chosen an escort who would in no way remind him of the girl who had ripped his life apart.

Tanned and sloe-eyed, Kona was the heartbeat of the president of the textile company for which Howard worked. She wasn't particularly beautiful, but she thought she was. When she came to the job site, every employee paid her obeisance. Her ears were laden with rings that jangled tinnily, waggery lurked in her expression, and Howard tagged her as a woman with the wiles of a snake charmer. He knew about worldly women, and he convinced himself that he had no interest in her. He wouldn't be snared by any woman. Nevertheless, she was a diversion, and that's what he needed.

On the night of the party, Howard was received at the door of Mr. Wantu's imposing mansion by Kona herself.

Her perfume, mixed with the scent of lilac blooms, created an intoxicating fragrance. Pinning a boutonniere to his lapel, she took his arm and signaled for the coach retained to take guests to the riverboat.

"It is a perfect evening, is it not, Howard?"

"It is, Miss Wantu."

She gave his arm a familiar pat. "Please call me Kona."

Ah, the chicanery has begun, Howard told himself.

The ride to the river was without incident, the conversation trite and shallow. Howard hoped it would stay that way. As he surveyed the crowd gathered on the wharf, he saw that Kona's evening gown, fitted and risqué, was modest in comparison to many of the others. His mother would blush at the indecency. But why should he think of his mother at a time like this?

"I hope that I may have the honor of a dance with you," Kona was saying.

"I'm not a dancer," Howard chuckled. "Your lovely feet would be crushed by my clumsiness, I fear, Miss Wantu."

"Just Kona, please," she reminded. "But, of course, you won't object if I leave you for a swing or two?"

"Oh, not at all! Dance all you want with whomever you wish."

Heels beat a staccato rhythm on the gangplank as skirts rustled and girls tittered. Here were the city's elite, flaunting their wealth in finery and jewels. Howard felt sorely out of place but willed himself to blend with the boisterous revelry. This he could only accomplish by pushing his mother's face—and her prayers—from his mind. He was ill at ease until the boat cleared the moorings; then he relaxed. Even if Elizabeth backtracked, she would never find him here.

After a seven-course meal of the finest caliber, the revelers spun into a gale of activity. The band Mr. Wantu had hired for the occasion struck up rollicking music. Tables were cleared and chairs shoved against the ropes. Then the whole deck became a whirl of flying bodies. Howard stood by the masthead and watched, hoping that no one fell overboard in the frenzy.

Eventually, Kona advanced from the sea of faces, casting Howard an upward glance; it was a look both inviting and seductive. Howard bent in the middle and brushed the tips of her fingers with his lips. "I am quite content, and you should continue your dancing," he suggested.

"This noise is giving me a headache," she complained. "Let's go down to Papa's office where it is quieter." She pulled Howard along through the din.

When they were in the stateroom, she closed and bolted the door. They were alone. "We can get better acquainted here away from the bustle of the crowd," she said, her voice breathy. "I tire of boring parties and dancing. Don't you?"

What would she say if he told her that he had never been to a dance? That, in fact, his straight-laced upbringing precluded dancing and drinking?

"Tell me about yourself. You're different." Had she read his thoughts?

What Howard *didn't* want to do tonight was talk about himself. He had come here to forget. "I prefer a better subject than myself," he demurred.

She looked into his eyes. "Howard, you are not having a good time. It is written all over your face."

"Oh, I am having a grand time!" It was a woeful protraction of the truth, but Howard tried to sound convincing. "You just don't understand me."

She took a step toward him. He took a step backward. "I must know one thing, Howard. Have you a sweetheart somewhere?"

The question angered Howard. What business was it of hers? What right had she to prod into his personal life? He opened his mouth, scalding words ready. Then he closed it hastily; he almost forgot that he was talking to the boss's progeny. His high-ranking position with a growing company must not be jeopardized by provoking Kona. She had her father twisted about her finger, and she could have a man fired.

Perhaps Kona realized she had riled Howard, for she now tried to pacify him. "My father likes you, Howard." She touched his hand with her long, glossy fingernails. "In fact, he has great plans for you in the company. It will benefit both of us to forge a friendship. Now tell me about yourself." It was a demand.

"What do you wish to know?" Howard struggled to keep his voice at a normal pitch. "My age? I'm twenty-five. My background? I'm an only child, born and bred in the state of Texas. My father is dead, my mother a widow. And, no, I don't have a sweetheart!" The last words were flung out, not without resentment.

"That's good news, Howard. I've one more question. Are you religious?"

How could he tell her that bitterness had driven a wedge between him and his God? How could he deny that his roots were planted deeply in the Word of God and regular church attendance and that he had miserably strayed from his upbringing? What words could describe his longing to have fellowship with the Master again as he once did?

"Answer me, Howard." Another demand, harsher this time.

"No." *I once was.* He wanted to say it but didn't.

"No what?"

"No, I'm not religious."

"Good. I could not cope with a religious fanatic. Religion is a crutch. It was invented by stodgy parsons for the weak and the ignorant.

"Now let me tell you about myself. I am twenty, and Father has been asked for my hand in marriage five times. However, you are the only man he has ever considered for a son-in-law. He says you have extraordinary potential. You're brilliant and willing to learn, perfect material to handle his business when he is gone."

The room became small, stuffy. Howard needed air. "I don't plan to marry. Ever."

"You can change your plans, Howard Brinnegar. Have you ever heard of love at first sight? Well, that's what I experienced the day I laid eyes on you at Father's plant. And let me warn you: What Kona wants, Kona gets." She gave a brittle laugh. "In this case, a marriage license with my name on it might be worth a million dollars to you."

Howard didn't want Kona. He didn't want a million dollars. He wanted out of the cloistered stateroom. If he could get topside again, he promised himself, he'd leap over the rails and swim to shore. Better to drown than be caged with this temptress. He would not be conned into marrying any woman for any amount of money.

Kona moved closer. Her perfume smelled like poison. "Hold me closely, Howard . . ."

No! Had he screamed the word aloud, or was it still

bottled inside, threatening to rupture the lining of his
soul? Howard's mind grappled and searched. This girl
might decide on a "Potiphar's wife" maneuver. How could
he make his escape?

A story in the Bible about David and what he did in a
dire crisis popped into Howard's consciousness. David
pretended to be a lunatic, slobbering and making sense-
less marks on the door. If David could pretend himself out
of a tight spot, so could Howard Brinnegar!

"I'm—I'm sick, Kona." He made a retching sound and
grimaced. "Seasick. I—shouldn't—have—left—the—
fresh—air. It's the swaying of the boat. Unless I can see
stationery objects on the shore—lights, buildings, trees—
I will faint."

"Oh, my dear Howard! I'm so sorry! But I will stay with
you, darling. Forever." She caught him about the waist.

He'd heard those words before: *I will stay with you
forever.* They came reverberating back from the distant
past, chasing him, haunting him, wounding him. But *she*
hadn't stayed with him. *She* had left him. . . . He must flee
that awful memory! If he didn't, he would lose his mind.
He had come to forget, and it hadn't worked. He remembered every wretched detail as if it were yesterday.

Howard carried his pretense a step further. He stiffened his back, rolled his eyes upward, and slid to the
floor. When Kona unbolted the door and ran for help, he
suddenly "regained" consciousness and fled back to the
deck, welcoming the sight of a drunken mob.

For the rest of the evening, he ignored Kona, and
when the boat docked, he disappeared into the night.

On Monday morning, Howard found himself without a
job.

FIVE

NEW TERRITORY

Just before Dorchan's train reached Kansas City, it slowed and then came to a standstill.

"What's the problem?" Roxie's impatient voice hectored the porter. Her eyes harbored a sleepy, impudent look. "Did we run out of coal?"

"The bridge that spans the Missouri River has been damaged. We're stalled for repairs."

"How long will we be here?"

"Depends," answered the man.

"Depends on what?"

"On when we can get new cross ties. Could be a week or more."

Dorchan heard, and her heart plummeted. Oh, for solid ground and a soft bed! She had exhausted her resource of energy; she was spirit weary. It had become increasingly difficult to keep Destiny, bored with the rail car's confines, occupied. "I want to play in the sunshine and freshen air," she whimpered. "Can't we go back to Granny Mary's? Please?"

For five miserable days, they sat. On the sixth day, Roxie took her luggage and left with one of the shifty-eyed young men on the work crew. The porter, watching her exit, shook his head. "A lost one, that," he muttered.

Nor did Roxie return.

For two more days, they were hobbled. Dorchan conceded she couldn't have coped without Elizabeth. Destiny spent hours with the woman who had an uncanny "grandmother's touch." Elizabeth created a realistic replica of a doll from her handkerchief, invented dozens of attention-holding fairy tales, and played games with Destiny. The child's favorite was "Hully-Gully Handful," a guessing game to determine which of Elizabeth's hands held a hidden coin.

Destiny needed Elizabeth. But then, so did Dorchan. *Is history repeating itself?* she wondered. *Will I attach myself to another mother figure as I did to Mary Wickerton? Must there be a series of heart-wrenching partings?* Was her self-sufficiency so fragile that she would fall into the trap of dependence over and over? Had her fifteen miserable years in the orphanage so bereaved her of surety that she must seek it from an outside source forever?

Elizabeth spoke little of her own life, past or present. She seldom mentioned her son except in soul matters. God, she said, had made her a promise of his salvation, and God's grace was sufficient. Her faith seemed unflappable.

Time limped on in stops and starts, but with the bridge repairs completed, they finally made it to central Texas. At Garden City, Elizabeth hired a stagecoach for the remaining few miles to her home. It was Dorchan's first coach ride, and although the vehicle was musty with imprisoned heat, she liked it better than the train. Tacked on a side panel was a small, framed map detailing the route. Thin lines represented roads and small squares portrayed villages. Stage stops and a timetable informed passengers of their whereabouts. The chart gave one the feeling of definition rather than drifting.

"Puddin will have something for us to eat," Elizabeth said. "Puddin's first and last thoughts of the day are food."

"Puddin?"

"Puddin is my housekeeper. Howard insisted when he left home that I keep Puddin with me. I told him I would be quite all right alone, but he said he'd not rest a minute for worry if I didn't have someone around the place. He sends Puddin a check each month to keep an eye on me.

"Actually, Puddin has been with us all of Howard's life. She was his nanny. He gave her the nickname, and it stuck. He loved her bread pudding. Puddin was a slave who didn't know what to do with herself when she was freed after the war. We offered her a home and an income. Of course, she didn't want money, but my husband insisted on paying her. She's been worth her weight in gold."

"See the flowers, Mommy," interrupted Destiny. The coach's curtain, fatigued and faded from its effort to keep the sun at bay, was looped back, and Destiny pressed her nose to the window. "They're all pretty like a rainbow."

Indeed, Dorchan had never seen such a medley of variegated colors as the fields of wildflowers that flanked either side of the road. "All the flowers have names," Elizabeth said.

"What are them?" the child asked.

"The yellow and pink ones are buttercups. The wine-colored ones are bachelor's buttons. The red ones with the brown middles are Indian paintbrushes. The violet ones are sweet Williams and the blue ones, bluebonnets.

Do you know your colors yet?"

"Most I do. I know red and yellow and blue. My eyes are blue, and my hair is yellow. And when I'm hot, my face is red.

"Mommy, aren't you glad we choosed Texas?"

"Yes," Dorchan answered, and with sudden perspicuity she knew she had made the right choice. There could not be a more delightful backdrop for the drama of her life. Paul Wickerton and his duplicity seemed a universe away. She sat forward eagerly as if to reach ahead to her exciting new future. She could see it. She could feel it. . . .

A winding road led to Elizabeth's rural home, and the beauty of the plant life followed them all the way. Puddin met them with a face-splitting, white-toothed grin. "Lawsy mercy, Miz Liz. It's time you be getting back!" she babbled. "Puddin is getting worried and lonesome! And look who is this precious chile?" She beamed down on Destiny, who impulsively flung her arms around the ample housekeeper. "And do she like bread puddin', I wonder?"

"Her name is Destiny, Puddin. And a grand child she is!" introduced Elizabeth.

"A belonging-to-you grandchild, Miz Liz?"

"I wish!"

Puddin was everywhere at once, a whirling cyclone, helping to unload, chattering, serving. She brought cookies and milk for the travelers.

"Make ready the big upstairs bedroom for Dorchan and Destiny, Puddin," Elizabeth instructed.

"Next to Master Howard's own room?"

"Yes."

"Don't go to any bother," cautioned Dorchan. "We will

only be here for a few days. Just until I can find work and get a place of my own."

"Aw, lawsy, now," the housekeeper's face fell. "I was hoping you'd stay on and on, Miz Dorchan. We need a bitsy Destiny around this big ole place here. That there winding bannister is made for chiles to slide on. Ain't been no slidin' there since Master Howard was in knickers."

Puddin showed Dorchan to the dormer quarters, a room papered with a dainty flower pattern. Dorchan caught her breath at its loveliness. Hooked rugs sprawled on a polished wood floor beside a four-poster bed with an appliquéd quilt in a rose design. Blessed by a good light from the glass-paned window, a low table kept reading material for a nearby rocking chair. And Elizabeth had invited her to her *humble* home?

"I'll bring you a tub and hot water," Puddin called. "After all that trip, you'll want a bath."

The offer took Dorchan aback. "I'm not accustomed to being waited on."

"I likes spoiling folks," grinned the maid. "That's my specialty."

Destiny darted into the room. "Please come and see something, Mother. Something very pretty."

"In a minute, Destiny."

"Please, *now*, Mother." When a grown-up importance demanded, Destiny called Dorchan "Mother." "Pretty please. It's only a little space away."

The appeal moved Dorchan to the door. She followed Destiny to a room left of the stairwell where the child pointed to a painting on the wall. "There! Isn't he pretty?"

Dorchan stared, transfixed, at the portrait of a prince-ly young man whose favor tattled that he belonged to

Elizabeth Brinnegar. The man's eyes . . . She could not pull her attention from them. And with her observation came a strange certainty that she had seen this man somewhere before. But where?

The child bounced off again, and Dorchan unpacked, leaving the wedding dress in the portmanteau. She could hear Elizabeth and Puddin talking downstairs, catching up on the news of their days apart.

"How was Master Howard, Miz Liz?" Puddin pried.

Elizabeth gave an audible sigh. "He is still running from God, Puddin."

"God'll cotch him!" Puddin said. "God can run mighty fast when He's after a man. God has long legs and long arms."

"Yes, God will corner him. I don't know what it will take—"

"God knows what dose of medicine he be needing, Miz Liz. Howard be a good boy. He have a heart as big as the sky. Look what he do for ole Puddin and for his maw every month!"

"But it seems his big heart is only becoming harder. He didn't want me reading the Bible to him or praying with him this time. Why one would turn from God instead of to God when trouble comes is more than I can understand. But it seems that is what Howard has done."

"Master Howard is forgetful to count his blessings."

"That he is. He has locked in on the past and forgets that he has good health, a wonderful job, and a home to which he can come anytime. He can't see the forest for the trees, so to speak."

"That Cassie did a number on him when she left, didn't she, Miz Liz?"

"Yes, Puddin. He has been unable to put her into God's hands and go on—"

Elizabeth's son was engaged or perhaps married, and his companion left him, Dorchan concluded. *And he blames God.* She didn't know Howard Brinnegar, but she knew all about hurting. She could help a hurting mother pray for her hurting son. Focusing on someone else's problems might help divert her attention from her own wounds.

The screen door slammed, and Destiny's Boston slippers drowned the rest of the conversation below. But Dorchan had heard enough to arouse her curiosity and to activate her sympathy.

Destiny, who had been exploring the house and its premises, shattered Dorchan's reverie. "Mother!" she panted. "Our friend has a bathtub with *feet*. And Catty-kit has babies with their eyes closed. And—" she stopped. "Don't you think this is better than getting a daddy and wearing the pretty white dress?"

"Perhaps so."

"What will you do with the white dress?"

Dorchan hugged Destiny to herself. "We'll put it away, and someday you will wear it, my sweet Destiny." Her smile braided happiness and regret together.

SIX

A JOB

The inn was made of milled lumber and painted white. Two large trees, their branches forming a leafy arch, stood on either side of the front door. Hanging from a low branch, a wooden swing invited lovers to sit under the moon. Romantic bushes of graybeards grew nearby. Dorchan tried not to notice.

She let herself in and met Emmett Randleman, the proprietor, face to face. His sideburns and the edges of his rusty hair were graying, but his face looked no more than fifty and was a place where a smile would feel at home. He put Dorchan at ease with his gentle manners.

After a brief interview, Mr. Randleman gave Dorchan a job at the inn, assigning her a room. "If Elizabeth Brinnegar recommends you, that is enough for me," he said. "She's as good a lady as heaven ever made."

Fortunately, Dorchan didn't hear the conversation in the parlor that evening. She wouldn't have opened a trunk.

"Emmett, why didn't you just tell the girl we had already filled the position and didn't need anyone else to work right now?" A perfect portrait Parmalea made as she stood, shoulders erect, her bejeweled hand on the curve of the settee. Except for the chronic pout lines about her mouth, she was beautiful.

"I . . . couldn't, Parmalea."

"It makes history that your tongue is useless," she scorned. "You've turned away dozens of applicants before."

"This one was . . . different." The coach house manager rolled the sleeves of his denim shirt a round higher, exposing strong, muscled arms. His jaws, like the rest of him, were square.

"She's skin and bones like the next."

"Yes, but she said she felt the Lord directed her here."

"So that's the password? All a tramp has to do to get a job at the inn is hear a voice from the sky?"

"Parmalea, you are bordering on blasphemy. The girl is no run-of-the-mill sort. She is sincere and in need. She has a child—"

"Emmett Randleman! Don't tell me you hired someone with a snotty-nosed, sneezing kid to spread germs all over the rooms of our patrons!"

"I run this inn. I'll do as I please." He didn't raise his voice.

"And you'll go bankrupt if we keep taking nonpaying boarders. We'll have no rooms left for travelers."

"If God sent her—and I believe He did—then He will provide for us. I dare say she won't eat enough to keep a sparrow alive. She's a slight thing."

"And likely too weak to lift a chamber pot. What shall I have her do?"

"It's up to you to find a job for the people I hire."

"Where is she from?"

"I don't know. I didn't ask. Elizabeth Brinnegar spoke a good word for her, and that's all the credentials I need."

"Certainly, certainly. Someday you'll hang yourself with the rope of that widow's words. To hear you tell it, Widow Brinnegar wrote the Ten Commandments. She should have added an eleventh: *Thou shalt not hire anyone below thirty or over fifty to work at thy inn.* How old is this new girl?"

"Around twenty, I'd guess."

"What happened to her husband? Why isn't he supporting her?"

"I didn't ask."

"You are taking a daring risk, Emmett. A girl so young is apt to flirt with our customers."

"She isn't the flirting type. A man would no more consider trifling with her than he would with a white-winged angel. It's as if she is holy. She makes you want to talk clean, think right, be a better man just being in her presence."

Parmalea gave her husband a questioning gaze. "Emmett, I believe you have gone religious."

"When I get religion, I want the kind that girl has."

"What is her name?"

"Dorchan. Dorchan Brown."

"And the kid?"

"Destiny."

Parmalea groaned. "Destiny. What an ignorant name for a child!" She turned to leave, her heel coming down hard on the oak floor. "Which room did you give her?" she called back.

"The top southwest."

"That's the coolest room and with the river view," she objected. "She can't have that one!" But Emmett's retreating back gave evidence of his dismissal.

In her spacious room, Dorchan emptied the trunks while Destiny spiraled in giddy circles. "Mommy! Our new home is wondrous!"

"It is. But if you don't slow down, you'll get dizzy." Dorchan placed her buckram-covered Bible on the roll-top desk, a hymnal beside it. Indeed, it was good to have a room and a job. *I've never had a real home*, she reminded herself. *This is the closest to home I've ever had anywhere.* With these accommodations, perhaps the deep longing within her heart, hidden from everyone, that she could have had a mother to dress her in pink and put wide, stiff ribbons in her hair, would be less acute.

When Dorchan had set the room to order, she walked to the window and drank in the panorama of a verdant valley stretching to the banks of a meandering ribbon of water, a tributary of the Lampasas River. Across the rill, a mossy rim rock provided a miniature waterfall. Small animals moved about freely, enjoying nature's paradise. Embowered in God's extravagant handiwork, the sweep below brought an inexplicable peace. Grackles circled and called, dark silhouettes etched on the clear horizon. Heaven was a duck-egg blue.

Was it only a month ago that the chapter of her life logged Paul Wickerton's cruel abandon? The years she had spent in Illinois now seemed a work of fiction. The real book had just begun. She had a friend, employment, and living quarters so lovely that she compared her lodging to a mansion even before she should enter the pearly gates. She gave a tiny shiver, wishing she were cut in thin slices so that she might explore her world in a thousand directions at once. Were she Destiny's age, she would run for joy, too.

Turning from the window, Dorchan saw herself repeated in the oval mirror fastened to the tallboy. Dark circles badgered her eyes, signs of recent duress, but they would soon be gone. Here she could rest. Heal. Forget.

Self-consciously, she pressed her hands along her faded skirt to smooth it. It had seen many wearings, but it was her best. Now she regretted that she had not sacrificed more hours at Mary's machine to provide herself a better wardrobe.

Mr. Randleman had told Dorchan that she should meet his wife the next morning, at which time she would be given work instructions. For all this luxury, no assignment would be too taxing. Dorchan was surprised that Mr. Randleman hired her knowing that she had a child to care for. What she didn't know was that Elizabeth Brinnegar had talked with the proprietor, assuring him that she would keep the child if a problem should arise.

When she tucked Destiny into bed, Dorchan bent to kiss her forehead. "Sleep, baby. Mommy wants to talk to God and thank Him for His goodness."

"And for Mr. Rand?" Destiny shortened Mr. Randleman's name to fit her vocabulary.

"Yes."

"And for friend Elizabeth?"

"Yes."

"And for Puddin?"

"Yes."

"And for Catty-kit?"

"Yes."

"And for—"

"Close your eyes now."

"And tomorrow we work?"

"Tomorrow we work."

"I will help."

That night, Dorchan slept hard, free of dreams. Sunlight spilled over the sill in a cloudless morning when she awoke. She hurried Destiny into a day gown and planted a bow in her mound of curls. Then taking the child's hand, she started down the staircase, pausing when she heard voices.

"If the new girl plans to sleep all day, I must speak to Emmett. I won't tolerate a lazy employee. Have you seen this young woman, Betta?"

"Not this morning, ma'am, but I helped her get her baggage to her room last evening."

"What does she look like?"

"She looks a mite young to have a youngster."

"Is she pretty?"

"Pretty isn't what you notice first even though she is fetching. It's an angelic look that does you in."

"Don't speak foolishly, Betta. Have you seen an angel?"

"No, ma'am, but—"

"Then do not presume to make speculation of which you know nothing. I suspect she is anything but an angel. A runaway, perhaps. I dare say she left her husband, if she ever had one."

"Excuse me, Mrs. Parmalea, but she doesn't seem the kind that would up and leave a man. I suspect he's dead."

Parmalea ignored Betta's defense. "I still can't figure why Emmett hired another hand and with a child to boot!"

"We can always use more hands, ma'am. Mr. Randleman prides himself on good service. That keeps people coming back, and we have more customers every year it seems to me. The vacation season hasn't seen its peak yet."

"But we don't need *her*. She will just be an extra expense."

"I wouldn't be disputing the Lord, ma'am. Mr. Randleman said the good Lord sent her."

Parmalea sighed wearily. "And Emmett gave her the best room in the whole inn!"

"The Lord's children deserve the best."

"Since she's so angelic, she likely won't unfold her holy wings to be of any earthly value whatsoever!"

It may have been a creak on the stairwell. Something made Parmalea turn around to find Dorchan and Destiny, the targets of her disparagement, poised like statuettes on the steps.

"Doesn't the nice lady like us, Mommy?" Destiny's voice was frightened and thin.

"Shh, Destiny," Dorchan whispered, putting a finger to her lips. Then facing Parmalea unflinchingly, she stated, "I will do anything you ask, madam." Dorchan's calm manner unhinged the pampered Parmalea. "I am accustomed to hard work with little consideration of my personal limitations. And I shall change rooms immediately if you prefer."

"Oh, mercy, no!" Terror crossed Parmalea's powdered face. "Emmett is the final word around here. Where he put you, you shall stay. Any mention of it will only drop me in a patch of nettles!"

Standing above Parmalea on the landing, Dorchan analyzed her in one glance. The lines about her mouth told a story of spoiled dissatisfaction. The way she held her head revealed her poisonous pride. Selfishness gleamed from her gray-blue eyes, and her dress exposed her craving for attention. Dorchan, carrying in her bosom a soul of compassion, saw beneath it all a shallow, unhappy woman who needed life's richest gifts, and she blinked back tears of pity. Better to have been reared in an orphanage than to be obsessed with materialism.

"Where shall I begin?"

Parmalea, stripped of her aplomb by the tearful eyes of a three-year-old child, turned to the cook in her confusion. "Have her empty the chambers and scrub the floors, Betta. And change the linens, of course." She turned and ran.

Betta watched her go, a slow grin broadening her mouth.

"That . . . is Mrs. Randleman?" questioned Dorchan.

"It *was*," choked Betta, suppressing giggles. "She left in a hurricane like her dress's tail was afire, didn't she?"

"Is she ill?"

"She must be. I've never seen her act so skittish before."

"Should we see about her?"

"She'll recover."

"What are your orders for me? Which room should be first?"

"The guests are still resting and wouldn't wish to be disturbed this early in the morning. We've made little signs for them to post on their doorknobs when they are ready for their quarters to be cleaned. That will be your cue. There will be no work for you until after breakfast."

"And my daughter may go to the rooms with me?"

Betta looked from her to the child.

"She will not bother anything; she is a well-minding child."

"And I'll help Mommy." Destiny hoisted her small

64

shoulders so as to look taller.

Still Betta made no response.

"Will there be a problem?"

"It's just that you and the child seem too pure and lovely to empty slop jars and spittoons."

Dorchan laughed; she liked Betta. "I've never dodged work. I was given the dirtiest jobs at the orphanage."

"You worked at an orphanage?"

"I was reared in an orphanage. I am an orphan."

"You have no family?"

"None on this earth. But God is my Father. When I was fourteen years old, He adopted me into His family."

"Praise be!" rejoiced the cook, her beam exposing dimples manufactured by years of cleaning up the inn's leftovers. "Then you are my sister! I've prayed many an hour for the good Lord to fetch someone here to help me show these folks the way of salvation."

Dorchan pondered what Betta said. Had she a special mission here? "I've never tried preaching. But I can pray," she offered.

"Your life is already preaching. Why, I've never seen Mrs. Parmalea so unraveled as she is today."

"I hope that I always may be a Christ-like example." Dorchan turned to go.

"Breakfast is at eight o'clock. And what is your first name?"

"Dorchan." She inclined her head toward the child. "And this is Destiny."

"I'm just plain ole Betta. Like I tell the diners, 'Betta for the cook when you are hungry!'" Dorchan joined her light laughter, feeling that she had just acquired another friend.

As Dorchan descended the steps, she heard Betta mutter, "Well, I never—! Mrs. Parmalea acted plumb scared of that innocent angel-lady."

SEVEN

TRIALS

In the drawer of Betta's mind, there were no locked diaries; secrets were not sacred to her. She said what she thought, seldom thinking before she spoke. That was Betta's way.

"Mr. Randleman should never have married that heathen of a wife," she told Dorchan one day when the proprietress had been especially rude. "If pride is a germ, she is a sick woman."

"Mrs. Parmalea is not a Christian?"

"What does the Good Book say, ma'am? It says that a tree is known by the fruit that hangs from its limbs. The way that woman crops and frizzes that hair, paints up that face—and all for the benefit of the gentleman boarders—doesn't go along with fruit the good Lord would pluck. Her fruit is *rotten*."

"What about Mr. Randleman?"

"He used to be a church-going man when his first wife was alive. And I think he's not far from the kingdom now. Oh, he takes his toddy now and then, but this wicked second wife drives him to it, I'll warrant. Like I say, he made a miserable mistake when he married her, and so soon after he lost Mrs. Laura.

"Now, his first wife, Mrs. Laura, was as lovely a thing

67

as God ever wrapped up in skin. She loved flowers, and she loved animals, and she loved children. And above all, she loved God. Why, she could have been the mother of Moses. Or Jeremiah. Or the apostle Paul. She had a gracious spirit. She helped every hurting thing, great or small. Everybody worshiped her, especially Emmett Randleman. But when she was gone, it left such a lonesomeness on his soul that he grabbed the first thing that came along.

"The whole town knows how Mrs. Parmalea chased him mercilessly. She was a milk and egg peddler from Georgetown who heard that Mr. Randleman's wife died. She came here and squatted until he proposed. Snagging the inn owner went to her head; she got pridey. Of course, she supposed that he had money, and money was her passion. When she learned he had nothing but the inn, she went sour on him. But by then her maw didn't want her back, you see, so—"

"Betta!" The bark was Parmalea's.

"Sounds like Betta better get back to work, Dorchan." Betta's voice lowered to a conspiratorial whisper. "But don't you worry over her daggers. She can't fire you."

Truly, the one fly in Dorchan's ointment was Parmalea. The woman disliked Dorchan and had no tolerance for Destiny. Antonyms they were, Parmalea and Dorchan. Travelers whispered of it; drivers noticed. Dorchan's gingham dresses contrasted glaringly with the oyster silk of the proud lady's imported frocks. And much to Parmalea's chagrin, Dorchan was the house favorite.

To make matters worse, Parmalea resented the attention that Destiny drew. She was a charming child, a heart stealer. The more the proprietor's wife ignored the child, the more the guests patronized her. The situation gave Dorchan reason for concern.

Public opinion is probably all that saved Dorchan and Destiny from Parmalea's injustices, for had the "boss lady" mistreated them, the whole establishment would have risen to arms, led by the capable personage of Betta. Betta had never feared jeopardizing her position; cooks like Betta were in high demand. The inn would not survive a week without her. Parmalea knew it, and so did Betta.

Another strike against Dorchan's finding any favor with the madam was that Mr. Randleman took a liking to Destiny. Fearing that the child would grow weary following her mother from room to room all day, Emmett devised ways to entertain the youngster. He took her riding in his wagon and built her a sandbox. He doted on the child and doubtless would have kept Dorchan in his employ simply for Destiny's company.

Destiny loved the outdoors. "I like the squirrels, I like the weeds, and I like to make winding roads in my sandbox, Mommy," she told Dorchan. "I like winding roads."

"Why winding roads, dear?"

"'Cause they are long, and they take you lots of places and make you be glad to get home at the end."

Mr. Randleman allowed Dorchan one day a week off work. When he gave her a choice, she chose Sundays so that she and Destiny might walk with Elizabeth to a small log church about a mile out in the grove. Here the worship drowned memories of tired feet and Parmalea's hatred. The stench of unemptied pots lost its nauseous influence over her stomach; the steamy heat of the laundry room was forgotten. She embraced this day as her primrose amid thistles. After lunch, Elizabeth insisted that Dorchan have a "Sabbath's rest" while she watched the child.

"I will keep Destiny while you work, Dorchan," Elizabeth suggested on more than one occasion. "It will be better for both of you."

But Dorchan was adamant in her decision to keep the child with her. "She isn't your responsibility, Elizabeth. She is mine. Thank you just the same."

The middle of summer brought scorching weather and additional guests, necessitating a trip to Austin for supplies. Mr. Randleman was gone for several days, and Parmalea took advantage of his absence to make life nearly unbearable for Dorchan. When Destiny overturned a glass of milk, Parmalea screamed at the child. She criticized Dorchan's appearance, calling her "frumpy," and complained that her work was unsatisfactory.

Dorchan kept Destiny near her at all times, raising protests from the child. "Please let me stay with friend Elizabeth and Puddin and Catty-kit," she begged. "I'm tired of sloppy jars and stinky smells and that woman who don't like me." The child's dragging reluctance slowed Dorchan's work, stretching the hours of labor late into the day and occasioning yet more scolding from the taskmistress. Parmalea laid upon Dorchan twice the chores of any other employee.

The truth became clear to Dorchan: Parmalea wanted her to leave. So why not oblige her? *Why did I ever think I could succeed in making a living for myself and Destiny without being a burden to someone like Mary Wickerton or Elizabeth Brinnegar?* At nineteen, she had been too young to assume the responsibility of a newborn in response to a dying mother's plea. Children needed families. A father. A grandmother. She was doing Destiny an injustice. But, oh, how could she give up the child for whom her very life existed? Without Destiny, she would have no attachment, no reason for being, no purpose for living.

A tearful Dorchan went to her room and pulled the trunks from beneath the bed. Where would she go? What would she do? Would she never stop running?

Betta found her there. "I have a rip in my apron, and I came to see if you can—" she stopped. "What is it, Dorchan?"

"I'm . . . I'm leaving."

"Leaving?"

"Yes."

"Mrs. Parmalea has upset you, hasn't she?" Betta helped herself to a chair. "Now, Dorchan, you listen to me. You can't just leave without a good-bye to Mr. Randleman. He has been kind to you. It would be unfair for you to take the child away without a proper farewell. Mrs. Parmalea hates children, but Mr. Randleman loves them. And this one has taken a piece of the man's heart. He's a lonely man, Dorchan, and it would hurt him deeply if he should come home and find you and the child gone without an adieu."

"I can never please Mrs. Parmalea."

"Nobody can please that heathen lady. Now, dry your tears and see if you can help me mend this gash in my uniform."

"Have you a needle and thread?"

"I have a sewing machine up in my room, but I don't know the first thing about it. My mother left it to me."

71

"You have a sewing machine?"

"Yes, but a lot of good it does me!"

"I can operate a sewing machine! I made a living for three years by sewing."

"Bless you! Come on up with me, and we'll uncover the contraption."

Dorchan had never been to Betta's room, and the cramped quarters under the slope of the roof depressed her. "You should have my large room, Betta!" she cried. "You were here before I. It isn't fair—"

"No, no. Say no more. Mrs. Laura let me choose my room, and this is the one I wanted. It is high up, it is quiet, and I'm not bothered here." She moved a large basket from the top of the treadle machine and stepped back. "I don't even know how to open the thing."

With the skill of an ace, Dorchan threaded the machine and repaired Betta's apron, rocking the foot treadle back and forth evenly. "This makes me feel useful," she said, flooded by memories. "I sew with my heart."

"Sewing is your talent, Dorchan. I don't know why you are mopping floors."

"I thought God sent me here," Dorchan sighed. "But I can't take it any longer."

The prospect of telling Mr. Randleman good-bye brought dread, and Dorchan pushed from her mind the tearful separation of Destiny and her friend Elizabeth. It would be worse than leaving Mary Wickerton.

However, when Mr. Randleman put in his appearance, Betta intercepted him at the barn. From her window, Dorchan could see the two talking earnestly. Betta was no doubt preparing Emmett for the farewells. Dorchan was glad; that would make it easier for her. Betta had been her buffer on several occasions.

After the evening meal, Mr. Randleman called Dorchan into the parlor. Parmalea had gone to bed early, complaining of a headache. "Betta tells me that you are unhappy with your job," he said not unkindly. "If it is a matter of finances, I will raise your wages."

Dorchan hesitated. How could she tell this generous man that money wasn't the problem? Or even the distasteful work? Or the long hours? But that it was, veritably, his heartless wife? Physical burdens she could endure, but it was the mental and emotional abuse that threatened to break her. "My wages are sufficient, sir." She didn't look up.

"Betta also tells me that you are a professional seamstress. She suggests that you should be sewing instead of scrubbing. Frankly, I didn't know that you were scrubbing, but you are not to mop another floor or clean another room."

Was he displeased with her work, too? Would he fire her before she had a chance to resign?

He hurried on, "The inn needs a facelift. The chairs in all the rooms need new antimacassars. The windows could use new lambrequins. We could do with fresh pillow slips, table covers and napkins, as well as tea towels. Betta should have told me of this need long ago. Our fine clientele deserve fine appointments. Is it within your ability to make these items on Betta's machine?"

Dorchan raised her eyes, and in them glistened a new light. "Oh, yes, sir!"

"Then that will be your assignment, beginning tomorrow. Take your time. You will sew but six hours a day.

Then you may help Betta with the serving of the evening meal while I dine with Destiny on my knee. Is that agreeable?"

Parmalea's lack of civility fled from Dorchan's mind. "Oh, yes, sir. Quite."

"I am even thinking into the future, Miss Brown. Betta said that you made garments and hats for a clothier. My long-range plans are to convert one of the rooms in the inn into a dress shop. You and I could split the profit from the business and could do well. We have a lot of wealthy travelers who overnight with us. You could sew at your own leisure, of course. How does that sound?"

"Too good to be true, sir." Dorchan's world whirled.

"Then I shall send you to Austin on the morrow for fabric. My driver will see to your safety there and back. Take your little daughter to see the big town. I will earmark funds for a special gift for her. Is her birthday past or future?"

"I . . . I'm afraid I don't know her exact birth date, sir."

"You don't remember the birth of your own child?"

Dorchan flushed. The man would think she had taken leave of her senses. "I— Well, you see, sir, she isn't my child by birth. She was very small when I got her three years ago in October of 1871. She will be four sometime in the late summer or early fall."

"You knew her mother? She was a relative, perhaps?"

"No, sir. Do you remember the terrible Chicago fire?"

"Yes . . . I . . . do."

"As I was fleeing down an avenue, a mother dropped the baby into my arms from an upper story, imploring me to take her. I was only nineteen, but I supposed God had put her in my charge for a reason. That's why her name is Destiny."

"I see." Mr. Randleman dropped into a pool of silence.

"I hope that she will be no further problem. I'm sorry about the milk she spilled on your wife's sleeve while you were gone. I offered to launder the garment—"

Eventually the man spoke again. "You are a brave lassie, Dorchan. Destiny has never been—nor will she ever be—a nuisance. She is a blessed gift from God, and if you will allow me, I will see that both of you are cared for."

"Only if I can earn my own way, sir."

Mr. Randleman tiptoed away from the subject. "Oh, and remember two things about serving tables, lassie, and you'll do fine," he counseled. "Smile, and keep the cups full."

That night Dorchan's head swam with patterns and ideas. Sleep vanished. She fashioned day gowns and evening dresses with hats and gloves to match. She coordinated colors and sketched mental diagrams. Her own business? A shiver of gladness caught her about the shoulders.

She laughed aloud. And she didn't care whether or not Parmalea, nursing a headache in the room below, heard her.

EIGHT

A Bad Report

Awakening, Howard Brinnegar corralled his thoughts with a tight rein and tried to remember where he was. Why was his body sagging on a gray cot, every joint screaming against its hardness?

Oh, yes, now it was all coming back to him. . . . He had walked east from the Kansas City Union Depot where the town thinned from business to residential. Sandwiched between these two worlds, he had found a dingy stucco boardinghouse with a flat roof onto which other appendages had been plastered over the years, disfiguring the whole. It was the cheapest lodging he could find.

Kona had put him here. She had sabotaged every effort he made to find employment in St. Louis. If she couldn't have him, she wanted him out of her sight, out of her town. To this end she plotted. In this she determined to succeed.

Absorbing the first shock of finding himself without a job or a paycheck, Howard had worried none at all. He was young, strong, able-bodied. He would find a better position than the one he had been relieved of. He would show Kona. He would show the world. He was sure of it.

Nor did the initial bevy of rebuttals shake him. He

plodded on cheerfully, sure that another day would bring better news. After two weeks of beating the bushes with no results, his optimism began to wane. Still another unproductive week threw his confidence into a nose dive. He was getting nowhere. Some devious plot lay behind this great exclusion.

For himself it wouldn't have mattered, but Howard was a principled man, armored with the old-school opinion that men should take care of the women in their lives. He had supported his mother since the death of his father two years ago. If he didn't provide for her, he would be no man at all. However she might provoke him, whatever her idiosyncrasies, she was his mother, widowed and his financial responsibility. Puddin, her housemaid, was his dependent, too.

His small savings wouldn't stretch far; then what would he do? Or rather, what would they do? He couldn't let them down.

When his rent came due, he dared not spend another cent to sustain himself in a fruitless environment, so he promptly moved without direction or plan. It was warm weather, and he figured he would manage with the sky for a roof. To remain in the city of St. Louis would be financial suicide. Someone—and he was sure he knew who that someone was—had undermined his chances of earning another dime there. It was time to move on.

He hitchhiked west. However, the hit-and-miss means of transportation cost him so much precious time that he decided to board a westbound train and stop at the larger cities along the way to look for work. Any job would do.

Missouri wasn't blessed with large towns. The closest metropolis proved to be Kansas City, and there he disembarked to begin his search. Not a soul did he know, and he found housing was neither plentiful nor economical in this boom town. There were pilgrims living in sod huts.

The best he could do for lodging was a stuffy back room in a cheap tenement house, airless and dank. One smoky window overlooked a back alley where garbage spilled over wooden barrels and rodents hopscotched among piles of spoiled refuse, seeking a morsel of food. A good sense of smell wasn't a blessing; when the window was opened, the rancid odor was oppressive.

This morning, the room irked Howard. The uncomfortable bed irked him. The toxic perfume of the sewer irked him. He gave way to self-commiseration, being the object of his reflective deliberation. He didn't belong in this pigsty. He felt detached from everything about him as if he and his burden could fit nowhere.

A country boy come to the city, he hadn't really fit in St. Louis. And he surely didn't fit on this flat plain with its rangy buffalo grass and sunflowers. Maybe he would do well to go on to Dodge City, the new railhead for cattlemen. He could work in the stockyards. As a boy, he had loved to be around animals. He had learned they could be more considerate than people.

He longed for his mother's huge house, a large, old-fashioned structure permeated with love, laughter, and Puddin's puddings. There he could lay down this lost feeling.

Gloom enveloped Howard as he pulled himself from the bed and went to the stained washbowl to shave. A cracked mirror, which cut his face into an upper and a lower section, contorted his appearance but failed to distort the worry that wrote itself on his features. He tried to expel the prodigal's echo: *What am I doing in this swine pen when in my boyhood home there is a feather mattress and good food and . . . ?*

No, he couldn't go back. He couldn't return to the breath of sweet honeysuckle, the winding trail to the river, the places he had been happy with *her* before his heart was broken. Mr. Randleman would give him a job at the inn; Mr. Randleman had always liked him. But he didn't want a job at the inn. He wanted nothing to do with Salado or his past.

Howard's stomach growled for food. He had eaten all the greasy pork and cabbage he could tolerate at the boardinghouse. The prodigal's husks couldn't have tasted worse. He would find a cafe and there stanch his hunger with appetizing fare even if it meant a splurge of his dwindling resources. A gaunt and hungry man wouldn't make a good impression as a future employee.

Six blocks away he found a restaurant. That's where he met up with Roxie. She came through the screen door, jangling the cowbell tied to its spring. Busily devouring his crackers and buttermilk, Howard did not look up. He did not see the girl squint to adjust her vision to the cafe's interior then pan her eyes across the establishment. Like a nail drawn to a magnet, she moved toward Howard's table.

Her slippers, her handbag and her perky hat were red, brilliantly red. So were her lips. Her eyes, the color of English wood, fit well with her hair, a cascading black cloud. At first appraisal, Howard pegged her as artificial and haughty, a woman to be shunned if one's reputation was to be spared.

"Excuse me, sir, but haven't we met before?" Roxie lisped.

80

"I doubt it, ma'am. I have only been in Kansas City for a few hours."

"A gentleman as handsome as yourself cannot be easily forgotten."

Flattery, he surmised without effort.

"I know that I have seen you—"

"We have never met. I am sure of that."

"Then we must become acquainted, of course. My name is Roxie. And what is yours?"

"Howard Brinnegar."

"Brinnegar . . . Brinnegar. Now, where have I heard that name? Let me think." She pursed her lips, touching her temple with a painted fingernail. The sudden arching of her penciled brows preceded a little laugh. "Ah, yes! I know now. Do you know an Elizabeth Brinnegar?"

Howard started, dropped his spoon. "Why . . . yes. She is my mother."

"Ah, as I thought. The eyes are the same. That gorgeous gooseberry color!"

"And may I ask where you met my mother?"

"On the train." She toyed with a strand of hair, calling attention to its midnight blackness. "She was returning from St. Louis. She had been visiting with you, I believe. We would have become instant friends had it not been for another young woman traveling the same route." Roxie moved closer to Howard and lowered her voice for emphasis. "A little vamp. She pulled the wool over your mother's eyes."

"What do you mean?"

Roxie placed a chair dangerously near Howard's elbow. "May I sit close to you, please? I wouldn't want any other ears to hear what I have to say."

"I can't imagine anything concerning my mother that would be so private. Mother has always been open and honest—"

"Oh, but this is confidential. Immediately upon meeting Mrs. Brinnegar, I sensed that she was a gracious and caring woman. A nurturer. The girl of whom I speak—her name was Dorchan—presented your mother with such a tale of woe that her heart was stirred to sympathy. But everything the girl said was lies. I know. I am acquainted with the girl and her background. Dorchan is after money."

Alarm bunched Howard's jaw muscles. He hoped his mother was wise enough not to give away the money he sent her for living expenses. "You must tell me everything so I will have the complete picture."

"Gladly. Dorchan is an unprincipled alley cat who has a child without the benefit of a marriage contract, if you get the drift. Yet she convinced Elizabeth Brinnegar that the child was not hers but that she had adopted an orphan in an act of benevolence. The story was long and ludicrous, and Dorchan shed a few crocodile tears to go along with her fabrication. And that's all it took."

"All it took for what?"

"Your mother offered to take Dorchan and her fatherless child into her home. Just like that." Roxie snapped her fingers. "I heard her invite Dorchan to live with her, to make her home with her."

Howard pounded his forehead with the heel of his hand. "Mother has lived in a rural area all her life; she isn't versed in underhandedness. Although I have tried to warn her about shysters, I fear she is gullible."

"And her charity flies on the flagpole of Christianity, I

dare say." Disrespect and mockery met on Roxie's face. When Howard did not comment, she tried to cover her irreverence with, "It does make a difference when you've been around, doesn't it?"

Whatever Roxie's intended implication, Howard ignored it. "Well, that explains things a bit. In Mother's last letter, she mentioned a new friend and a child named Destiny."

"Destiny. Yes, that was the little girl's name." Roxie reached out and touched his arm. "Oh, you poor dear! I know it must concern you terribly, but you are here and she is there. There's little you can do about it. I say let the old folks take care of themselves and let us get on with the business of enjoying life. Do you plan to be here long, Howard?" She said his name in a particularly intimate way, lingering over the last syllable.

"I came here to find work, but—"

"Marvelous! I shall be glad to take you around and introduce you to some prospective employers. I know everybody. This is a lively town, really. New people are moving in every day. The parties do tend to be dull, though. Anyhow, they were until you came along. A gentleman like you can add spice to any social gathering. Which reminds me: my escort for tonight broke his leg. I will be most delighted for you to join me—" She used her eyes to their fullest advantage. Had it not been for her self-awareness, Howard conceded, she might have had a hint of charm.

"Thanks, but I must leave immediately. Since you've told me what you have about Mother's guest, I am convinced that I should hie myself on to Salado with all speed. Mother does have some valuables about the house, some heirlooms that must be protected."

"Oh, I didn't mean to imply that Dorchan is a thief, Howard! Only that she has led a morally decadent life and has been irresponsible with her virtue. I am sure a few more days won't make any difference—"

"I am a man who likes to attend to matters before they fester. I cannot settle my mind to a new job until I see this problem resolved."

The ruse Roxie had used to capture Howard had backfired. "At least you could wait until tomorrow."

"No, I shall go today." Howard pushed back his chair, leaving most of his meal untouched. He headed for the door without casting a backward glance at a girl who for once had not been able to change the plans and arrangements of a man to suit herself.

NINE

SEAMSTRESS

Betta's *Tailor's Gem* had been moved to Dorchan's room for convenience. Dorchan patted the machine. "You and I will show them, Gem. We'll have a rip-roaring business going before they can say 'Jack Frost.' We'll make dozens and dozens of beautiful garments." She felt seized, swept high by a mighty updraft. "We'll outfit the lovelorn, the brides, the hopeful mothers. You will help me earn enough money to buy a place for Destiny and me so we can be independent and happy."

When Mr. Randleman's driver took her to Austin to select material for the inn's appointments, she invested some of her own savings into yardage for a new dress for herself, a green crepe de chine that matched her eyes. She bought a copy of *Harper's Bazaar* for modern pattern ideas, then spent the designated funds on fabric to launch the special project the inn's proprietor had introduced: a dress shop. With a stock of thread, laces, braid, buttons, hooks and eyes, she had no doubts that her business would prosper. No qualms beclouded the horizon of her mind.

How time flew! After her six industrious hours of sewing for the inn, Dorchan managed a few spare moments to create her first dress for retail. A lovely outfit it was, sapphire blue in grosgrain silk. It boasted a fan-pleated skirt that fell over a narrow frill at the bottom. The collar was crimped to stand up around the neck, and miniature fabric roses added fanciness. Anxious lest she had overpriced it, she hung it in the parlor with its price tag also displayed. But before the day was out, the wife of Garden City's mayor bought it without even a quibble over its ghastly cost of seven dollars. Dorchan subtracted one dollar for material, leaving three dollars for her share and three dollars for Emmett Randleman.

Mr. Randleman refused the money. "You will need more supplies, Dorchan," he advised. "Until you get the business off the ground and running, you are to keep all proceeds from your sales."

"But Mr. Randleman, it was our agreement—"

He made a wall of his hands. "I insist. And anytime you need to make a trip to Austin, I will have a driver at your disposal." He closed the subject.

A week after the initial sale, a well-dressed woman called at the inn, asking for "Miss Brown." Betta went for Dorchan. "I am from back east," the woman announced with a sweet Pennsylvania accent. "My name is Helga Harper, and I am a personal friend of the mayor's wife, for whom you sew. I am in need of a new wardrobe, and I wondered if I might make an order."

"I'll do my best to please you," Dorchan nodded.

"Oh, I'm certain you will. I'm not that hard to please or to fit. The dress you made for Trudy is proof enough of your expertise." A friendly, chatty woman, she rambled on. "But isn't this a glorious part of the country? Its rare beauty makes one want to transplant to the south. It has been twenty years since I've seen Trudy. My, doesn't time fly? We grew up in the same neighborhood—Trudy, my sister, and I—and went to school together. What one of us couldn't think of, the other two could.

"I was a twin, you see. Being a twin is great fun, sharing a birthday and all. We didn't have the jealousy that plagues some twins; we got along perfectly. My twin's name was Velma. Well, when we grew up, Velma went west, Trudy went south, and I stayed put.

"When I realized that Velma wasn't coming back, I felt that a part of me had died. So I promised myself that someday I would make a trip south and visit Trudy. But what with taking care of my injured husband until he passed on, time got away, and I'm just now getting here. And what a reunion Trudy and I had!

"Then I learned that Trudy has this wonderful seamstress within driving distance. And is it possible, dear, that you can make a few extra dresses for me to take back east with me when I return? I like the southern styles. They're more bouffant, more romantic."

Dorchan hadn't been able to get a word in edgewise. That, she reckoned, would have been like trying to thread her sewing machine with the treadle going. "How long will you be here, Mrs. Harper?" she now asked.

"Well, I figure that since I was so long about coming, I might as well make it worth my time. I have no one back in Pennsylvania to worry over me. My plans call for six weeks or so. But if that isn't long enough—"

"I am quite fast with the machine and the needle. How many outfits did you have in mind?"

"Oh, five or six at the least."

"I'll take your measurements and start on them right away."

So came the orders, precipitated by word-of-mouth advertising until Dorchan's heart and hands were full and she had a waiting list. It looked as though her pockets would soon be bulging. Ere long, she would start looking for a house with a parlor large enough to serve as a show-room.

Her heart sang. Fresh energy flowed through her as she helped Betta serve the evening meals. She moved about gracefully, serving plates of aromatic food to the inn's numerous guests. She loved meeting customers, catering to their wishes, and she enjoyed working with Betta. Betta was one of those cooks with an intolerance for cookbook recipes. Her own version of plum pudding, caramel-capped with amber sauce, brought raves. As a result of these culinary arts, the inn's dining room never lacked patrons.

The new dress Dorchan had fashioned for herself, a princess sheath with a row of handsome buttons in a long, narrow line down the front, transformed her in both body and spirit. The first time she wore it, she caught her reflection in the looking glass and gasped, sure that the mirror exaggerated the effect of the color on her eyes. Had she been given to vanity, the dress may have mired her in that vice.

Parmalea cast envious eyes toward Dorchan, but her husband looked pleased. "Such a waitress is good adver-tisement for the hotel," he mused. "Dorchan is making an excellent hostess." His approving eyes followed her to the kitchen and back. "She is most efficient."

"She really hasn't been here long enough to prove her worth, Emmett. Hirelings usually work well for the first few days to make a good impression and collect their pay.

Then they slack off and laze around. But at least she gets on well with Betta. That's more than I can say for some you've hired in the past. And, mercy knows, we have to keep Betta, regardless of her incorrigible tongue and her religious fanaticism!"

"That's a pretty frock Dorchan is wearing this evening. I would be interested in knowing if she made it herself."

"It's not like you to notice clothes, Emmett. You never make favorable comments about anything I wear."

"I had a special reason for wondering if Dorchan made the dress herself. She has been selling a few garments commercially and doing quite well."

"She—what?"

"The mayor's wife from a neighboring town bought her first creation and spread the word."

"She is sewing on your time, and you've made no efforts to stop her? I should think that would constitute a conflict of interests and be grounds for dismissal."

"I gave her my permission to sew."

"Emmett Randleman! Have you lost your wits? There is no telling what a girl with Miss Brown's reputation might make for public display. I tell you, I won't have you self-destructing and taking me with you!"

"I make the business decisions around here, Parmalea. I had the inn long before you came into my life. The inn is my problem. That was the agreement when we married, remember?"

"I've never seen a man so bent on economical destruction. A firm built on indecent personnel is sure to come to naught. That girl is hiding a skeleton in the closet, and you are too blind to see it. She romped on your pity so you would give her a job. She pretends to be a Christian, but Christians don't lie. And she is living a lie."

"The Constitution gives you the right to say what you will, Parmalea."

"I will certainly have my say. You turn your head to impurity, and you've even attached yourself to the girl's fatherless child. I dare say Miss Brown is flirting with you behind my back!" She spat the words. "And you persist on believing her, don't you?"

"Yes."

"What reason have you to trust her?" The silence towered. Her look invited him to topple it with an explanation.

"What reason have I not to trust her?"

"Just remember one thing, Emmett," Parmalea's accusing eyes narrowed. "Skeletons get mighty restless in closets after a while."

TEN

PURSUIT

Paul Wickerton was angry with his mother, angry with himself, and angry with the world at large.

But mostly, he was angry with the woman he had wed. When she discovered that he hadn't a bottomless purse to indulge her whims, she dropped him and scampered off to greener pastures. She promptly had their marriage annulled.

The young man that Mary Wickerton had sent to the university was not the young man who came back. Years wasted there in riotous living had depreciated his mind, besmirched his soul, and deteriorated his body. His character, like a long neglected building, had crumbled to decay.

Paul had written to his mother for financial assistance, but her return letter brought no funds. How dare her to ignore his request! He was ready to give her a piece of his mind!

With no money and little inclination to earn any, the immature man headed for home, his thoughts churning. He could always go back to Dorchan. She had a penchant for dressmaking, and she would be glad to support him. A rather simple girl she was, easily fooled, but she might prove useful to him after all. How he would tolerate the kid, he didn't know. It would be his mother's tack to find a way to keep the brat out of his hair, off his nerves. It wouldn't be hard to convince Mary to rear the child, though. She was mawkish about the youngster.

He was angrier yet when he reached home and found that Dorchan had slipped from his grasp. It maddened him that the monthly income bolstered by Dorchan's rent was diminished, putting his mother at a monetary disadvantage.

"Where did Dorchan go?" Paul barked.

"I don't know where she went, but she left with a broken heart. The girl really loved you, Paul."

Paul exploded. "If you knew she loved me so dearly, why did you let her leave? You should have kept her here until you saw how my relationship with Aurilla would fare."

"But . . . I didn't know. You told me that you planned to marry—"

"Well, I didn't marry. I got to thinking about what you had said: that Dorchan was a home-style girl and as good as gold. You were right, I concluded, and the sensible thing for me to do was to come back home and marry her." Paul knew how to weave his lies with truth in such a manner that the truth protected the untruth. "Then I opened my eyes and saw Aurilla for what she was, pampered, self-centered, and citified. Not at all my type. We never could have gotten along. But now you've gone and spoiled everything by letting Dorchan get away!"

"Please be reasonable, Paul. You told me that you did not want Dorchan."

"And I suppose you told her that?"

"I said not one word to her. I didn't even tell her that

you planned marriage. However, I think she felt rejected when you were here for the holidays, and so she went away. I didn't ask her to leave or even hint that she move out."

"When will she be back?"

"She said she wouldn't return."

Paul, acting like a juvenile, smashed his fist on the table. "Which direction did she go?"

"I asked no questions."

"Did she go by stagecoach?"

"She went by train."

An oath fouled Paul's mouth, bringing a censuring look from his mother. "I can't believe you didn't find out where she planned to move! I thought you loved her enough at least to want to keep in contact with her! But I'll find her. I'll get on the train and stop at every depot until I do."

"You must never let her see your temper, Paul. It will frighten her."

"I'm no dunce, Mrs. Wickerton. I know how to woo a woman." He hissed the words.

"I trust you know how to treat one after she is wooed."

In no mood for a lecture, Paul disregarded the words. His stockpile of psychological weapons included silences and cold stares, armaments he knew would sting the most.

He saddled a horse and rode to town for a visit with the ticket agent. From the man he learned that Dorchan had boarded a southbound Pullman. Her destination was not listed.

Paul then talked his mother out of all the savings she had stashed for emergencies, promising to return with

Dorchan and the child, at which time, he said, he would make restitution. He would yet set things aright.

So hungry was Mary to see the child who had brightened her onerous existence for three years that she put up no resistance. Money couldn't bring her happiness; a daughter-in-law and a grandchild could. She had cried every day since Dorchan left. What mattered if she was broke as long as she could rock Destiny, tuck her into bed, and feel the warmth of small arms entwined about her neck? "I will ask God to help you," she said.

"I don't need God to help me, Mother. I'm big enough to handle this myself. Spare your prayers for the feeble-minded." Paul departed with full pockets.

The porter remembered Dorchan. "That's a hard name to forget," he said. "I know she went as far as Kansas City. We were throttled down there for a lengthy spell due to rail damage." He couldn't seem to recall whether or not she left the train at that point. "Is she a relative of yours?" he asked.

"Yes," lied Paul. "And I need to catch up with her, for there is an urgency at home."

Paul's patience wore thin before the first day fell off the calendar. "Is this as fast as this crate can go?" he bellowed at the brake man. "I could walk faster than this!"

"You're welcome to walk," was the man's retort.

Life was unfair, Paul steamed, for denying him a pedigree, riches and unmitigated leisure, for obliging him to run after a common girl like Dorchan. Why couldn't he have been born to wealth? To power? To aristocracy? He roamed from car to car, cursing under his breath. That night he tossed his berth into a twist of knotted sheets. This trip was necessary, of course, to please his mother and to keep a bead on her assets (such as they were). Dorchan could be dropped anytime a better arrangement developed.

At the Kansas City terminal, Paul gathered his traveling bags and looked about. A motley crowd congested the depot. Miners with picks and axes, loggers in picturesque costumes, homesteaders in calico dress and poke bonnets, grim-eyed, long-bearded mountaineers with pistols at their waists, and city-bred tenderfeet. The river of newcomers all yearned for frontier adventure or the opportunity to grab land in the west.

Where should he start to look for Dorchan? At a millinery shop, doubtless. He had seen so many of her patterns that he could spot them in a store window with one eye closed. But first he needed a drink. A strong one.

Standing on the wooden platform in attention-getting garb, watching passengers come and go, was Roxie, who had haunted the depot every day that week in hopes of ambushing Howard Brinnegar on his return. She wasted no time in slithering toward Paul, laying a bejeweled hand on his arm.

"I see that you are searching for someone, sir. I am quite well acquainted with the populace of Kansas City, and I might be able to help you if I may know for whom you are seeking."

Paul liked what he saw. Bold eyes. Red lips. Crow black hair. He liked the spirit he felt, too. "Actually, I'm looking for a Dorchan Brown," he said, "but I find it a great pleasure to meet someone as lovely as yourself."

Roxie's smile was as fake as if it had been chalked on a slate. "Dorchan? Why, I know Dorchan. We came to Kansas City on the same train. You are, in fact, the second young man in a week who has come in search of her." If her intentions were to discourage Paul from his search, it didn't work. The mention of another man unleashed a demon of jealousy in his bosom, but he hid it well.

"Who was looking for her?" He pretended nonchalance.

"Howard Brinnegar. Howard and I became very dear friends while he was here. I had a great party planned for him, but unfortunately, he was called away to solve some problem for his widowed mother. That's why I am here at the depot. I am expecting his return."

"What did he want with Dorchan?"

Roxie shrugged her shoulders in a careless fashion. "I dunno. I think he may have wished to marry her."

"She belongs to me! He has no right! I'll show him! I'll punch his nose!"

Roxie laughed, a high-pitched, false giggle. "Oh, you must be Paul Wickerton!"

"How did you know?"

"I heard that packsaddle kid of Dorchan's talking to a passenger on the train. She said you found another woman and stood Dorchan up at the altar."

"That's a lie! Dorchan ran out on me. And I'm daft enough to follow her and to try to coax her back."

"Ah, I call that love," mocked Roxie. "Or stupidity."

"Stupidity, no doubt."

"But I can't imagine anyone leaving a man as easy on the eyes as you." Roxie winked. "She must have had oatmeal for brains. And with her reputation! I'd think she would be glad to get anyone to give her child a name."

"Do you know where Dorchan is?"

"I do."

"Please give me her address."

"She doesn't live here. She traveled farther south into Texas," she sneered, "to join the other tumbleweeds."

"Tell me where to find her in Texas."

"I can't tell you. She went to a quite remote area. But I'll be glad to go with you and show you where she lives," Roxie said. "Truthfully, I've forgotten the name of the place. However, I'm sure I can find it once I'm in the area."

"I prefer to go alone. Give me some general directions, and I'll find her."

"You would never be able to find your way alone. Texas is a huge place, and a part of the way must be traveled by stage. I will take you there."

Paul frowned. This Roxie girl could mess up his well-laid plans. He already had one perfidious female to his credit, and he didn't need another. "Thanks, Roxie, but I don't need your help."

"Well and good, but why don't we forget about Dorchan for the time being and let me show you around Kansas City? You must be tired of the gruel they serve on trains. Isn't it the pits? I know where there's a lovely cafe with sumptuous food and the best wine around."

Paul's raging thirst and weak will cast him into Roxie's trap. He never knew when she sprang the latch. Hours later he awoke in a cheap brothel, owner of a splitting head and a penniless wallet.

Alarmed, he looked about. There was a dirty mat beneath him and a sooty ceiling overhead. What had happened to him? Where was Roxie?

Staggering to his feet, he splashed cold water onto his face from a chipped water bowl and went in search of the girl. Should he denounce her or thank her? Had she helped him, kept him from arrest in his drunken stupor, or had she taken advantage of him in his inebriation?

He found Roxie seated in a booth at the cafe where his imbibing had begun. "Paul!" She seemed genuinely surprised to see him. "Where did you go last evening? We were having a carnival! I went to the powder room, and when I returned, you had disappeared."

"I . . . I don't remember much," Paul admitted.

"I am afraid you overindulged in the wine."

"I was very thirsty. But I have some bad news."

"Bad news?"

"I was robbed during the night. My money is gone."

"Robbed? Where were you?"

"I took a room at the Dockside House."

"Oh, Paul, I should have warned you. That isn't a reputable lodge. It is no place for a gentleman like you. I don't wonder that you lost your money. Just be thankful you didn't lose your life!"

"Now, how will I get on to find Dorchan?"

"I have money. Remember, yesterday I offered to go with you. That offer still stands. I will purchase our tickets, and we'll be on our way. You mustn't worry. We will find your sweetheart."

ELEVEN

INVESTIGATION

What bends and turns the road of destiny takes is rarely exposed to mere mortals. It is often a winding, twisting path, overarched and obscured with the ordinary.

Ironically, Howard Brinnegar arrived at his mother's house on a Sunday afternoon, Dorchan's sabbatical with her friend Elizabeth. He was met at the whitewashed gate by a slip of a girl who stood no taller than the hedge of summer climbers that bloomed in spendthrift effusion along the pickets.

This, then, is the child that Roxie told me about, the fatherless child whose mother is taking advantage of my own widowed parent. Howard was glad he'd come; he would put a stop to the travesty. His meeting with Roxie had been providential.

"Hi, mister!" chirped the youngster, standing immobile to analyze him. Her innocent eyes gave his stomach the feeling he'd topped a hill too suddenly. "Oh, you are the beautiful man in the picture upstairs next to our bedroom! I look at you every time I climb the stairs. And so does my mother. You must belong to Granny Elizabeth."

Granny. Inwardly, Howard groaned. Things were worse than he had imagined. He'd arrived none too soon.

"Do you live here?" Howard asked, unable to hone the

99

edge from his voice.

"Oh, no! We live at the inn. My mother has a nice dress shop there. We only come here to go to church with Granny Elizabeth on Sundays. And we stay for dinner with her and Puddin. Puddin cooks the bestest custards in the world! What's your name?"

"Howard."

"I'm Destiny." The child gave a tiny curtsy. "And my mother's name is Dorchan." She clapped her hands together. "And, oh, Granny Elizabeth will be *so delicious- ly* happy to see you—just like my mother would be glad to see me if I was growed up and gone away for a long, long time."

In a surprise move, the child reached up and caught his hand. "C'mon. I'll take you to her. I know the exact chair she'll be sitting in. I'm glad you came before my nap time."

In vain, Howard tried to extract his hand. Destiny clung to it doggedly.

"To whom are you talking, Destiny?" At the door, Howard came face to face with Dorchan, who had started out to check on her chattering daughter. She drew her breath in a small gasp of astonishment and took a step backward.

"Don't be affrighted, Mommy," Destiny cheered. "This is beautiful Howard whose picture we admire every day. He has come to see his mother, Elizabeth. Won't she be gladsome?"

Dorchan, pink faced with embarrassment, raised her eyes and stammered an apology for her child's behavior. The action caught Howard off guard, and his heart did a crazy somersault.

The young lady standing before him was nothing like he had imagined. She fit none of his preconceived ideas. Roxie had drafted her on the easel of his mind in muddy colors, a moocher, brash and sinful. With her true eyes and blushing face set in a frame of gorgeous spice-colored hair, she seemed quite harmless. The light hung in her glorious tresses and turned the mass to alluring flame. He wondered what would happen if he dared to reach out and touch it just to feel its luxurious softness.

Then reality hit. Hard. He had been abandoned by one girl, and he could not let it happen again. He would not let it happen again. His heart, sequestered under lock and key, had almost escaped. Almost, but not quite. He had caught it in time and returned it to its prison.

"Howard!" Elizabeth leaped from her chair and rushed to the door. "Is it really you?"

Dorchan took Destiny's hand and pulled her aside, allowing mother and son a joyful embrace. "We'll walk back to the inn now, Mrs. Brinnegar," Dorchan said. "You will want to spend time with your son."

"But, Mommy, I wanted to—"

Dorchan hushed Destiny. "We will come another time, Destiny." She hurried the child away, contravening Elizabeth's insistence that they stay and visit.

Why Howard did not want Dorchan to leave he could not explain, but he said nothing to encourage her company. He was human, he was lonely, and he was jobless—and he could be fooled. Best let the woman depart so that he could properly warn his mother as he had come to do. With Dorchan out of his sight, he could better disparage her, dislike her.

"My dear, dear Howard," Elizabeth crooned, leading

him to a chair beside her own, "I trust that you have come home to stay! I have felt in my prayers that St. Louis is having a negative effect on your bruised spirit. A city is such a wicked environment—"

"I no longer live in St. Louis, Mother."

"Is it true?"

"I lost my job."

"Then you *are* home to stay!"

"Mother, you know that I could never be happy here where I met and courted Cassie. Everywhere I look, I see her yet. The path to the river. The porch swing. The garden. For so long, I kept thinking she would come back. . . ." He paused to brush away a tear. "A broken heart mends slowly, if ever. I really loved her, and she left me. I shall never fall in love again! I can't chance it. I won't chance it." The empty words sounded as though he were trying to convince himself.

"Life must go on, Howard."

"I *will* try to settle somewhere closer so I may visit more often as you grow older. Please forgive these last few months, Mother. They haven't been easy for me. But then, they haven't been easy for you, either. I was wrong to let bitterness overtake me. When Cassie left me, she took my heart and everything dear, and soon we lost Father. But I still have you and Puddin. For that I can be thankful. We get so embroiled in our grievances that we forget our blessings."

"I haven't missed a day praying for you, son. God has given me some precious promises, and I will be standing on them come Judgment Day. But there, let's not talk of past woes. Let's enjoy our time together. Can you stay for a few days at least?"

"If memory doesn't bring me to complete prostration, I will stay until I can find my way. Oh, Mother! I can close my eyes and see Cassie with her lips turned up at the corners, ready to smile! Or I can see her eyebrows raised in serious contemplation. Then just before I recapture a complete picture of her, she turns her back and walks away—"

"I know that you adored Cassie, Howard. We all loved her and hoped that you would be blessed with a long and happy marriage. But that didn't happen. I pray that someday you will love again—"

Howard was shaking his head vigorously. "I haven't the heart to try again. Time only solidifies the resolution I have made. What if I should gamble and lose a second time?"

"Trust, Howard. You must have faith."

"How can I?"

"Forgive. Forgiveness brings faith. Forgive Cassie. Forgive life for hurting you. Stop blaming God."

Silence, punctured only by the ticking of the grandfather clock, hung in the room like heavy smoke as Howard thought over what his mother had said. She was a wise and godly woman. Maybe he hadn't forgiven. . . .

He changed the subject, forcing the issue from his mind. "This girl who was visiting you, Mother. Who is she?"

"Dorchan is a young lady that I met on the train en route home from my visit to St. Louis. She happened to be traveling south in search of work. I suggested the inn. Emmett hires hands by the dozens. I recommended her, and she got right on. And a good hireling she has made; he is pleased with her. She has been a lot of company to me, and I worship her child."

"What happened to her husband?"

"Dorchan has never been married."

"Don't you think you are putting your good name at risk by taking in a stranger with a history of loose morals?"

"A history of loose morals?"

"I met a friend of hers in Kansas City. She tells me that this girl lacks virtue and that she has been quite promiscuous."

"Your friend could not have been talking about Dorchan. Dorchan is chaste of body and spirit."

"Is it possible that you could be misguided, Mother? Let me ask you a question. Have you lent or given the girl money?"

"Had she asked, I certainly would have. But she has no need to beg or borrow. She is quite self-sufficient. As an orphan, she has earned her own wage since she was fifteen. A lazy bone would starve to death in her body! She is one of the most hard-working girls I've ever known. Just ask Emmett."

"And no one here knows that her child was born out of wedlock?"

"Her child wasn't born out of wedlock."

"You just told me that she had never married. Now you contradict yourself."

"Is there a law, Howard, against a single woman rearing a motherless child? Dorchan took the baby at a dying mother's request and has made enormous sacrifices to care for her. She would give her life for the child. If that is not noble, I don't know the meaning of the word."

"How can you be sure that her story is true? I have heard otherwise."

"My judgment of character has always been rather accurate. I prefer to believe that Dorchan is a true-hearted girl. She is a born-again Christian, and she has given me no reason to doubt her."

"I shall do some checking on my own. I don't want the good Brinnegar name to be injured by a wolf in sheep's clothing."

TWELVE

THE CUSTOMER

On Monday, Dorchan measured Helga for the dress-making. Assisted by a corset with stiff stays, Helga had a diminutive waistline, giving her clothes the best possible frame to look classic. Any seamstress would enjoy such a model who, past her prime, was still befriended by a slim and youthful form.

Helga took great delight in leafing through Dorchan's pattern books. "Can you make all of these?" she asked.

"With the proper material, yes. I like trying to make the dresses look exactly like the pictures."

When the pages of the publication stood still, Dorchan waited for Helga's exclamations. "Oh, look at this, Miss Brown! A dress with a side-draped moiré over-skirt." Or, "I've never seen a more elegant gown!" And then, "Velma would have loved this one. Velma had good taste in clothes."

Then she would start to chatter, going into extensive detail about her family members who had all made their exit to heaven. "I know I talk too much," she apologized. "Have you noticed, Miss Brown, that people who live alone tend to overdo the conversation when they get a chance to say something?"

"Your stories interest me."

"But you have work to do."

Work was Dorchan's panacea. She'd never had a problem keeping her mind on her sewing, but of late she was amazed to find her thoughts distracted. They kept drifting to Howard Brinnegar. He had been to the inn to visit Emmett Randleman, and she had caught a glimpse of him out the window.

The portrait of Howard displayed in Elizabeth's upstairs room, the first in Dorchan's mental picture album, was now flanked by other pictures. Howard swinging an axe with powerful strokes, attesting to his boyhood years in the wood country. Howard's tanned arms piled high with oak logs for Betta's six-lid cook stove. Howard lifting quiet eyes to the distant river. . . .

Dorchan picked up her scissors to trim a pattern and stopped. Did she measure a half inch or an inch?

In service on Sunday, she had watched Howard, listened to his deep, sonorous voice join the others in singing the hymns. He had many of his mother's characteristics. He was kind. He was reverent. He was polite. But in spite of Destiny's pleadings, Dorchan had kept her distance; she no longer took dinner with Elizabeth on the Lord's Day.

Howard had given her no special attention, no reason to hope that he cared for her. In fact, except for a slight nod when his mother stopped to chat with her after church, she felt she was invisible to him. Although Destiny tried to gain his favor with every ounce of her childish charm, he seemed impervious to her sorcery.

How long did he plan to stay? On the one hand, Dorchan wished he would leave. She sorely missed the visits to Elizabeth's house. On the other hand, she desperately wanted him to stay though she did not peel the wrappings off her emotions to find out why. All she knew was that her heart pounded foolishly when she saw him.

Did Helga say she preferred buttons or hooks?

To settle her thrashing thoughts, Dorchan walked to the open window. A scissor-tail chased a hawk, tormenting him. The scene brought no peace, for she was as tormented with her own unnamed hunger. Something pecked at her mind, refusing to let her rest. Any reminder from the past could shift a dull ache into a throbbing pain.

Men's voices below the window arrested her attention. "I will pay you well, Howard." The words belonged to Emmett Randleman.

"I can't stay, sir. You know how I feel when I am here. I see Cassie at every turn, and it is like a knife cutting into my heart—"

"But if you could, just help me temporarily. This is my busiest time of the year, from now through Labor Day. My driver quit without a notice. His brother suffered a heart seizure, and he left to help the family. I will hire another driver as soon as I can find one."

"Parmalea would not be happy with me."

"Parmalea will find something to grouse about. Don't mind her. This is between you and me."

"What will the work consist of?"

"A taxi service of sorts. The guests sometimes need to get to Belton and back. Or perhaps to Garden City. Then there are the supply trips to Austin—"

"Those I won't mind. They will take me away from here."

"Most often you will have a passenger."

"Company will be a pleasure, a distraction."

"A female passenger."

"A—*female?*"

"Yes. I have a very talented young lady working for me. With her ability to sew, she is bringing business to the lodge. Women come for fittings and stay for dinner. Word is spreading like measles. The mayor's wife from Garden City brings customers. Customers with plenty of money. Why, it has even been suggested that my seamstress go into the mail-order business! A visitor from Pennsylvania promised a host of clients from back east."

"And why must I take this seamstress to Austin with me?"

"That's where she purchases her fabric and notions. She buys only the best. I dare say she'll make us all famous." His slight laugh held pride.

"Who is this lady?"

"Dorchan Brown."

"My mother's friend? The one with the little girl?"

"That one. The child is adopted, you know. Dorchan has never been married."

"I see. I hope she won't mind a mute driver. I haven't much rapport with women."

"She won't bother you, Howard. She keeps her place well. If her trip takes more than a day, she has a room at the Central Hotel. Except for coming and going, you will not see her. Her only ambition is to make a living for herself and the child, and I'm trying to see that she gets that opportunity."

The voices drifted away with their speakers, and Dorchan realized she had not moved from her place by the window. Her feet were glued to the floor.

So Howard would be taking her to Austin. Joy came from one direction, anguish from another. They crashed head-on in her soul.

Did Helga want tailored ruffles at the wrist or a fan of pleats?

THIRTEEN

A CHILD'S PARABLE

Elizabeth had stood it as long as she could. Without the patter of childish feet tripping across the parlor floor or running up and down the staircase, the house was depressingly quiet.

"I'm plagued with homesickness for Destiny," she told Dorchan, imploring her to allow the youngster to spend the afternoon with her on Sunday.

"Please, *please*, let me go, Mommy," begged the child. "My mouth is crying for Puddin's custard."

"But you have company," Dorchan reminded Elizabeth.

"Company? Howard isn't company!" objected Elizabeth. "He is family. Anyway, Destiny won't bother Howard. He likes children."

So Destiny went home with the Brinnegars, and she set in immediately to bother Howard. She insisted on sitting next to him at the dinner table. *Too* next to him, Howard considered. She moved suffocatingly close, permitting no one else to serve her plate but the "beautiful man."

Howard didn't mind dishing up her potatoes or her smearing gravy on his best shirt. He didn't mind her candid grace that included Puddin's meal, Catty-kit,

Elizabeth, and him. It was her nearness that agitated him. He had spent months building a formidable wall against anybody or anything that could affect his emotions. He couldn't let a blonde-haired baby topple that wall, a child bound by fate to a young woman who put a choke in his throat when he looked at her. He wished his mother hadn't brought Destiny home with them.

After the meal, Destiny wanted to teach Howard to play "Hully-Gully Handful," and he pretended he had never heard of such a game, though he had tormented his mother to join in the timeworn riddle for hours when he was Destiny's age. He supposed he owed something to his mother for those monotonous yesterdays. The least he could do was entertain Destiny while Elizabeth helped Puddin clear the table.

"How does the game work?" he asked.

"I hide my eyes and don't peek while you hide something in one of your hands," Destiny instructed. "I won't know which hand has something, but I will knock-knock on one of them. If I knock-knock on the full hand, then I win. But if I knock-knock on the empty hand, you win."

"Hmm," Howard said. "I see that this is a most interesting game. How about if I hide a penny?"

Destiny danced about in a circle. "Yes, yes!"

In the fun of the contest, Howard forgot his resolve to remain aloof. Destiny was winning; she guessed correctly more than she missed. Some uncanny sixth sense seemed to guide her to the proper hand.

"You're peeking!" he accused.

"I'm not!" she refuted. "My guesser just works good."

After a while, Howard decided to tease her by slipping the penny into his pocket and presenting two empty fists.

But she had her own trick ready; she knocked on both hands at once. He threw back his head and laughed so hard that Elizabeth came rushing in to see what occasioned the merriment. Howard hadn't laughed so heartily in years.

"The joke is on me," he acquiesced. "I am up against a clever opponent."

"I could have told you so," Elizabeth said, making her way back to the kitchen. "That gal is nobody's fool."

"Both hands must never be empty at once," scolded Destiny in a preachy tone. "When there is nothing in both hands, it spoils everything. Without something to hold inside, the whole game is gone. And it's up to you, sir, to put the penny back into one of those empty hands."

From the mouth of babes. His life. It was empty. He had refused to refill it when Cassie left. Oh, what a parable the child taught! Best that he coax her back to the game; her sermons were too vivid.

But the game was over. Destiny was ready to talk. "Have you ever wanted something to be there, and it wasn't?" She looked directly into his eyes. What fiend of discernment made her drive the spike of bygone injustices into his crusted spirit?

"Yes," he said, for it seemed that she looked deeply into his soul and wouldn't be put off until he answered. "When I was a small boy, I had a dog that was my best friend. He was—stolen from me."

"I'm sorry, sir." Her sympathy touched him. "I had Granny Mary, and I was sad to go away from her. But it was like putting the penny in another hand," she held out her hands to demonstrate, "when I found Granny Elizabeth. With Granny Elizabeth, I am no more empty.

Maybe you could get another dog."

"I could never feel the same about another puppy." He dare not confess more. A mere child, however perceptive, would never know that Cassie was mixed up in the paradox of his story. It was Cassie who had stolen *his* heart and then left it mangled beside life's road.

"No, not the same, probably, but you could feel just as good in a different way. I know because I love Granny Elizabeth just as much as I did Granny Mary. And with Puddin, too, that makes two pennies in one hand!" She giggled.

"You're too smart for your pinafore."

"My mother made my pinafore."

Howard didn't want to hear about Dorchan. "Umm." He studied the toes of his boots.

"*She's* the smart one. Once she made a pretty white dress for herself, but she didn't wear it. We were going to get a daddy—and, oh, I wanted a daddy worser than anything—but he didn't want us, so my mother still has the white dress. She says I shall wear it someday when I am growed up."

As the conversation wrapped around Dorchan, Howard grew uneasy. He stood to his feet, reached in his pocket for the penny and dropped it into Destiny's hand. "For the winner of our famous game," he said.

"We'll play again sometime?"

Howard buckled the mantle of his resolve tightly about him. "I will be leaving before long," he said, "and I may not see you again. Now I have some chores to do. Please excuse me."

"Can I help you?"

"No, I'm going to ride into town."

He bolted toward the door and was gone. Nor did he return until after dark, until he was sure that the child who had scrubbed his conscience raw would be gone. He hoped that Emmett Randleman would find another driver soon; he was anxious to move on. He couldn't abide another day like today.

Elizabeth waited up for him. "I'm glad that you and Destiny had a good time this afternoon," she commented.

"Mother, I would like to ask a favor of you. Please do not bring that child back to play games with me," he said. "Keep her any time that I am working but not on Sundays."

"But I thought you were enjoying—"

"I did enjoy her, and it isn't that I dislike the child. But— Well, I can't let myself get attached to anyone, child or otherwise, yet. It's too soon. Please understand, Mother. I'm not ready—"

"I will honor your wishes, son, but we must all bow to God's will."

Now what did Elizabeth mean by that?

FOURTEEN

Two of a Kind

Roxie was well acquainted with men of Paul Wickerton's ilk. Such were weak-spined creatures, blown about by every wind of whim, clouds without water, worth little to themselves or others. Paul fit into the kettle of humanity with spoiled boys and men who considered themselves the most important, most interesting people in the world. No arm was stronger than theirs, no voice could contradict them. Roxie wasn't interested in a companion with this lack of merit. People like him were a penny a dozen.

Like all the girls of her genre who go for the spiritual jugular veins of the best men, Roxie had her bonnet set for Howard Brinnegar. He would be a true conquest. She would take Paul to Dorchan and set about to trap Howard for herself. The Howard Brinnegars were few and far between, a vanishing breed and worth pursuit.

The philanthropic deed of escorting Paul to Salado, supplying his needs with the money she had stolen from him while he was intoxicated, would give her trip credence. With her telltale tongue in Salado, she would be able to further denigrate Dorchan's name, bracing Howard's warnings to his mother. There was always a way to get where one wanted to be even if one had to resort to alternate routes.

"Are you planning to take Dorchan back home with you?" she asked Paul, who sat brooding by the window of the train. Paul had been in a black mood all morning, unconcerned with the lush scenery of the high plains that slid by.

"Most certainly," he snapped. "If the Brinnegar guy puts up a fuss, I will let him know—in a way that he won't forget—that Dorchan is my woman. I courted her for three years."

"Did you ever love anyone else?"

"I didn't so much as look at another girl!"

"And did Dorchan have the child when you first met her?"

"She did. But the child will be no problem. My mother is batty about her. She will keep the kid from under my feet. If Dorchan must choose between me and the girl, she will choose me, of course. Dorchan is madly in love with me."

"That I could tell when I met Dorchan on the train. She was grieving for you. I tried to divert her attention, to get her to work with me. I thought I had her persuaded, but she changed her mind."

"Dorchan left a good job. She supplied some nifty boutiques with her hand-crafted gowns. She also had a good home and a chance to marry me."

"I understood it was you who jilted her."

"It was all a silly mix-up, the misunderstanding being on her part. Dorchan is bad to jump to conclusions. I came home for the holidays tired, burnt out, and sick. The school was hassling me about my grades. I was so disturbed that I didn't give Dorchan the attention I should have." The whole structure of his story teetered on the

120

edge of collapse. "She requires a lot.

"Besides, there was this dizzy dame at the college who was chasing me, writing notes, leaving messages, driving me nuts. Mother found out about the girl, whose name was Aurilla, and blew things out of proportion. It was a fear complex on Mother's part. She was afraid that I would marry Aurilla instead of Dorchan, a foolish worry.

"Dorchan may have heard Mother and me arguing. I said something like, 'Oh, sure, Mother. I plan to marry Aurilla!' Pure satire. Anyhow, I went back to school without a flowery good-bye, and when I came home for the summer to wed Dorchan, she was gone."

"She'll be glad to see you. I dare say she left hoping you would follow her. That's a woman's way, to run and hide. Women love hide-and-seek games with the men they fancy. They love being chased. You'll get her back. I'll help you get her back.

"But let me give you some womanly advice, Paul. She may play the hard-to-get game at first. She may even pretend that she no longer loves you. It will all be a front. Don't be discouraged. Go slowly, and give it time." Roxie wanted plenty of time to capture Howard Brinnegar. "We will stay however long it takes. A week, a month, or a year."

"Oh, I'll get Dorchan back, you'll see, even if I have to drag her back to Illinois with me."

"No strong-arm stuff, Paul. Flies are caught with honey."

"I just wish I hadn't lost my money. I may need to buy candy or sodas or perfume."

Roxie knew how to handle the men she swindled. "I'll lend you some money, Paul. Just ask when you need it."

She puckered her lips roguishly. "I have plenty."

Paul and Roxie arrived at Salado Inn while Dorchan was gone to Austin. They asked for two rooms. "I've only one room left for tonight," Emmett Randleman told them. "It's a downstairs room, but there will be another open up tomorrow next door to it."

"You take the room, Roxie," Paul said. "I'll probably be up most of the night anyway. Dorchan and I have a lot to talk about."

Emmett eyed him warily.

Roxie opened her purse to pay for her room. "You do have an employee here by the name of Dorchan Brown, don't you? The last time I saw her, she was headed here for work."

Emmett hesitated.

"We are friends of Dorchan's," Roxie bluffed. "In fact, you may have heard Dorchan mention Mary Wickerton, Paul's mother. Dorchan lived with Paul and his mother for several years. We decided to stop by to pay her a visit. Mary sends Dorchan her greetings. And she sent Destiny a quarter, see?" Roxie held out a coin.

The proprietor was a hard one to convince. "Dorchan is out of town," he said crisply, "and I'm not certain when she will return."

"Oh, then I will stay in her room tonight!" conspired Roxie. "She wrote and invited me to stay with her any time I came." Turning to Paul, she nodded. "You can stay in my room tonight, Paul. I will sleep in Dorchan's room, and tomorrow we'll move into our own quarters."

"We will be here for a few days," offered Paul. "I have never been to Texas, and I'd like to look around a bit to see the country." Roxie saw he was on his best behavior;

she was proud of him. "And if there is any way I may help you while I am here, sir, I will be glad to do so."

Emmett's face softened. "That Dorchan is a lovely young lady, and her young'un has stolen my heart. I'm hoping she stays around a while."

"And by the way, sir, I am a friend of Howard Brinnegar," Roxie added as if it were an afterthought. "Does he happen to be around just now? He did work in St. Louis, but I understand he wanted to move closer to home."

"He is at his mother's."

"I met Mrs. Brinnegar on the train. I hope to visit with her also." Seeing Emmett's puzzled look, she dropped one eyelid in a slow wink. "We have some wonderful plans that may surprise everyone, haven't we, Paul?"

"This is a nice area for a honeymoon," Emmett said.

"That's good tidings," Paul responded.

He thinks we are marrying each other, mused Roxie, *but is he in for a shock!* "Where may I find Dorchan's room?" she asked.

"The top southwest, Miss—what is the last name?"

"Rail. Roxie Rail. R-a-i-l."

One of Roxie's greatest amusements was to spell words backward. She hoped the proprietor didn't turn the letters around. No one had been that smart yet. They would spell "liar," and that's what she was.

FIFTEEN

SHOCK

The supply trips to Austin gave Dorchan a break from her busy work schedule and from motherhood. Elizabeth kept Destiny, who had proven to be a poor traveler. Everyone benefited.

The drive was one of exquisite beauty; God outdid Himself in the stretch of terrain between Salado and the state's capital. A dozen shades of green carpeted the knolls and flats, thick and luxuriant. Although the bluebonnets had already seeded out, larkspur bloomed in abundance.

Once at her destination amidst the foulards, grenadines, gauzes, satins, and muslins of the dry goods store, Dorchan lost her cares in the delight of textures and prints. To her the emporium was a haven. Milling through masses of edgings, gimps, lace, and ribbons, she forsook heavier thoughts.

The city with its adobe and frame buildings spread along the Colorado River. A center of business for miles around, it boasted two banks, a barbershop, a drugstore, a hardware establishment, and numerous general stores. The main street fanned out to include eateries, hotels, dress shops, and the well-stocked dry goods market. Its populace possessed with southern hospitality, Austin was a true shopping pleasure.

This trip had been her first with Howard as driver. He'd settled in his seat with unmoving steadiness, his left elbow resting on the buggy's edge, his right hand holding the reins loosely. He had said little on the journey, but she hadn't expected much chitchat. Once, though, she caught him studying her out of the corner of his eye. When she glanced his way, he quickly turned his head away. She wished she could have a look inside his mind. He was baffling, sending ambivalent messages. However, he was constant in his politeness, helping her in and out of the buggy as any chauffeur would.

Had happenstance thrown them together, or was there a method to the madness? She couldn't still the racing of her heart when he was near. He made a handsome sight with the mist of the new morning glistening on his generous hair that afforded only one deep wave in the front. His broadcloth shirt fit well, giving credit to his broad shoulders. *I would like to make a shirt for Howard.* From whence did the thought spring? She had made all of Paul's clothing, but making a shirt for Howard would bring special fulfillment.

What must this man have suffered? And what woman with her senses about her would desert such a prince as he? Whoever she was and wherever she was, she had certainly succeeded in destroying the man's trust in women. Dorchan wished she could meet her to tell her what irreparable damage she had wrought.

Wasn't there a verse in the Bible dealing with an offended man? If her memory served her right, it said that such an injured one was harder to be won than a strong city. She wasn't trying to win Howard, of course. She had a business to build, a daughter to rear and to educate. If ever she did marry, however, she would like someone with the integrity of Howard Brinnegar. He had a strong chin, clear eyes, work-worn hands. He was as different from Paul Wickerton as light and dark. Paul found satisfaction in his own will, a trait of one who knew not God. Howard had known God; he had another spirit.

From a distance, now Dorchan could see the real Paul: self-centered, weak-willed, disrespectful. He would ever be a loser. She was glad she had not wasted the white wedding dress on a charlatan.

The shopping went well, and Dorchan arrived at the inn at mid afternoon of the second day, armed with bolts and bundles. Destiny would come to the inn for the evening meal with Elizabeth. To celebrate, Dorchan would wear the green dress she had made.

In her room, Dorchan looked about. She didn't remember leaving her bed unmade. What had she been thinking? She never left her bed untidy! And there was a strange odor of perfume in the air. Had someone come into her room in her absence? Surely not!

A mystery it was, but she hadn't time to dwell on it. She must ready herself to help Betta serve the evening meal, an assignment she enjoyed. A few people frowned upon girls who worked as waitresses, but Dorchan could see nothing wrong with honest work. And there was no one to reproach her anyway. The serving, as well as the sewing, was God's way of providing for her.

When she thought on God's provisions, she felt warm inside as though a screen had been removed between her heart and a fire. The future looked bright.

Betta greeted her enthusiastically. "My, I'm glad to see you back!" she gibbered. "We are full up. Every room.

And the dining crowds are growing every day. Oh, yes, and you had some friends come in while you were away."

"Friends?"

"From a long distance."

"I have no friends from a long distance except Helga."

"No, it wasn't Helga. It was a young man and a young woman. They didn't look like your kind."

"Do you remember their names?"

"I don't, but they were about your age."

Dorchan's brows knit to a ponder. "I can't imagine who it would be. A mistake, probably."

"The girl stayed in your room."

"In my room?" Then that accounted for the unmade bed, the sweet, floral smell of perfume. "She will be embarrassed when she finds that she stayed in an unknown person's room."

The tables were filling. Patrons laughed and talked, refreshed by the wholesome atmosphere devoid of drinking or smoking and by the decorative beauty of the centerpieces. Betta believed in snowy white tablecloths and fresh flower vases for each group.

Dorchan bobbed in and out, bringing tea, coffee, and juices while smiling, nodding, and refilling cups and glasses. The green dress made her feel alive, animated.

Elizabeth came to sit with Emmett and Parmalea, and Dorchan took the time to give her daughter a hug. "Mommy, Catty-kit's babies are big enough to run away now. They try to hide from their mother. But if they go too far, she grabs them by the hair of their neck and hauls them back—"

"Yes, dear. Mommy will talk to you later. We'll have a long talk when we go to our room tonight. Mommy is very busy."

Howard came in late to join his mother and the Randlemans at the already congested table. Chairs scooted around to make a place for him. Dorchan thought he looked wonderful in his fresh shirt and cravat. She had served him before and knew without asking that he would want coffee with cream and two dollops of sugar. This she supplied, brushing against his sleeve as she did so. A prickle ran up her arm.

Howard's smile was strained, but it was a smile nonetheless. "Thank you, Miss Brown."

"Isn't my mother lovely in her new dress?" Dorchan heard Destiny chant, and she gritted her teeth, darting back to the kitchen. Children were frighteningly unpredictable.

Emerging again with a china platter that buttressed a mountain of roasted potatoes, Dorchan was drawn by a magnetic force to look at two latecomers just joining the hodgepodge of diners. The man, hatless and composed, stood looking bemused while the girl's chocolate eyes searched for a vacant seat.

Seeing them, Emmett Randleman pushed back his own chair, arising to give them a host's welcome. "I hope that you are finding your rooms commodious, Mr. Wickerton and Miss Rail."

For an instant, Paul's eyes met Dorchan's and held.

"Dorchan!" Roxie blurted, and Paul made his way toward Dorchan with a stride of possession.

"Yes, my lovely Dorchan!" he intoned. "I found you! At last!"

Dorchan's mind sought only escape. Her legs turned to jelly beneath her. What was Paul Wickerton doing here? Had he married Roxie and then concocted some devious plan for her, too? She had to get away to winnow some sense from it all.

Quickly, she turned back to the kitchen to catch her breath and to conquer the battle that raged in her breast. But in her haste, she stumbled on the threshold, sending the ornate platter to the floor with a crash. Potatoes splattered this way and that. She struck her head on the door's facing and crumbled into a motionless heap.

"The dish! It is broken!" Parmalea gasped. "Our priceless platter!"

"Never mind the dish, Mrs. Randleman." Howard jumped to his feet, upsetting his chair. "Let's make sure the *girl* isn't broken."

"Mommy! Mommy!" sobbed Destiny.

Betta heard the commotion and rushed in, wiping flour-covered hands on her apron, forgetting her job in the scullery. "My poor Dorchan! What happened to her?" Uttering a mixture of concern and comfort, she turned to Emmett for an explanation.

"I don't know, Betta. Did she seem ill when she came to work?"

"No, sir. She was fit as a fiddle with twice the rosin."

"Was she sick on the trip to Austin, Howard?"

"No, Mr. Emmett. At least not on observation. She was in fine spirits and seemed rather to enjoy the trip."

"Should we send for the doctor?" Betta asked.

"Doctor's calls are costly," Parmalea intruded. "Emmett can't afford to pay medical bills for a kitchen helper's clumsiness."

"Take the money out of my pay," insisted Betta.

Dorchan opened her eyes and looked about. "I'm not hurt. Really. Just—just—"

Paul pushed through the crowd. "I will take her up to her room. Come, dear. We'll leave this place if you like. This very night. You are exhausted, and you shall not work here another hour."

Howard stood to one side, saying nothing. Dorchan found his eyes. "Please," she implored, "if I may be taken to Elizabeth's house—"

The man in Howard responded to a weaker vessel's plea. He knelt to scoop Dorchan into his arms, but Paul bumped against him. "Mister, this is none of your concern. Dorchan is my intended bride, and I shall care for her myself."

"No! No! It isn't true!" Tears budded behind Dorchan's eyes. "Oh, please, Howard—"

"She is irrational," disdained Paul.

"Irrational or not, she is my employee, and she will be given time to recover before you take her anywhere, Mr. Wickerton." Emmett's words were kind but firm. "Howard, take Dorchan to Elizabeth's house for recuperation as she has requested."

Howard lifted Dorchan into his hard, muscled arms. Roxie was at his elbow. "You are so brave and strong, Howard!" she purred. "Any woman would feel safe in your grip. Remember me? I am Roxie, your friend from Kansas City."

"I remember you." The words were as flat as soup without salt.

"I want to thank you for helping Paul's fiancée. But do beware. Dorchan is good at this sort of thing. She faints to get attention. Why Paul wants her, I wouldn't know, but he does. Love is a strange thing, isn't it?"

Howard strode away, leaving Roxie talking.

When the excitement had settled and they were back to their table, Parmalea raged to her husband. "I told you, Emmett, that the girl would be a liability. I knew she would not last through the summer. Those frail folk who come from up north cannot stand the searing heat. You will have to let her go."

"Work wasn't the problem, Parmalea, or the temperature. Something startled Dorchan and made her stumble. I saw the look of shock in her eyes. She will be all right when she has had time to pull herself together."

"Surely you don't plan to keep her after this evening's episode?"

"Only if she wishes to stay."

"We can't have a girl working here who breaks expensive dishes. Before long we will have no china left. That was our prettiest serving dish, imported from France."

"We'll see what the future holds, Parmalea. We don't have to make a decision today."

"Emmett, you are being downright ridiculous about this whole thing. Why the obstinate persistence to keep a frangible girl—and one with a child yet—when there are plenty of hearty others with more experience in coach house work? If you keep defending her, I will be persuaded that there is something going on between the two of you!"

"Parmalea! *No more!*"

Obviously, the woman knew the outer perimeter of Emmett's patience, knew how to push him there and no further.

She turned and stalked out.

SIXTEEN

GUARDIAN ANGEL

"I am quite well enough to continue my sewing," Dorchan insisted. "A bump on the head doesn't give one license to be idle."

It went unsaid but understood that she planned to stay with the Brinnegars until Paul Wickerton took his leave from the coach house. On this premise and at Betta's instructions, Emmett moved the *Tailor's Gem* to Elizabeth's home. He vouched, though, that Dorchan should keep her room at the inn. All would be back to normal before long.

But all did not go back to normal. Paul made a pest of himself, sometimes calling on Dorchan twice a day. If she was sleeping, Elizabeth refused him entrance. The man became adept at divining when Dorchan wasn't resting and demanded to see her. Howard held his peace but became a silent sentinel.

One day while Destiny was playing in the yard, Paul caught her by the shoulders. "You are never to come inside while I am visiting with your mother," he warned the child. Howard, on his knees and weeding the shrubs a few feet away, went unnoticed.

"If you do not obey me, I will cuff you. Hard." He slammed his fist in his open hand for emphasis.

"Granny Elizabeth won't let you do that." The small chin lifted to a defiant angle.

"Granny Elizabeth would never know it. And you must not call her Granny. My mother, Mary Wickerton, will be your grandmother. You are a spoiled brat, and when I marry your mother, you will get the hickory tea you deserve. If you don't do as I say, I will sell you to the Indians."

Destiny's voice quivered, tears near. "I'm ain't for sale."

Through the brush, Howard could see terror in the child's eyes, and his heart constricted. What demented soul did Paul Wickerton house beneath his jaundiced skin? Paul was no man; he was a bully. No real man would frighten an innocent child with such threats!

"Mother says she shan't marry you. The pretty white dress is for someone else. You didn't want us."

"Your mother *will* marry me."

"You aren't nice. God will give us a nice daddy."

With unconcealed contempt, Paul reached out to strike the child. Howard leaped from behind the bush like a coiled spring and caught Paul's hand in midair. "You will not touch the child." His interruption was so unexpected that for an instant there was no sound, no movement.

Then Paul jerked away and moved on to the house. A wild, mirthless laugh broke from his throat.

Angrier than he had ever been in his life, Howard walked down the path that wound itself to the river. It was none of his business if Dorchan married the louse, he told himself. His only interest was in protecting the child. He cared not a shred who Dorchan Brown married. Or did he?

When he had carried her in his arms to his mother's spare bedroom and she had thanked him with humble gratitude, he had known one fleeting moment of sweet anguish, the anguish of parting with her, the anguish of wanting to hold her forever close to his chest. He fought it. He denied it. He rejected it. But it clung like a burr to his spirit.

Floundering in a backwash of conflicting emotions, he tried to sift through the ashes of confusion for a grain of logic. Try as he might, he had not been able to unearth a smidgen of evidence to substantiate Roxie's gossip. Dorchan had not imposed upon his mother. She had given in little, thoughtful acts much more than she had taken. Not once had she asked for money or other valuables. Emmett Randleman was convinced that she was pure, true hearted. He had not found a wanton fiber in her being. Why should anyone wish to vilify her?

It frightened Howard to think what he might have done had that soul-scarred man, Mr. Wickerton, injured the child. Destiny had built a road directly to his heart though he'd tried to put up roadblocks. He hadn't meant for it to happen, but it had. To contemplate the mistreatment of the golden-haired cherub brought a wave of nausea. Children were to be nurtured and cherished and guarded.

Beside the tumbling brook, Howard sat on a stone and watched the minnows dart between the rocks. A restlessness roiled in his heart, an unrest he could not explain. He wished he could discover its fountainhead. He had been a good son, honoring his father and mother; he loved God and country, willing to give his life for either. Yet his life had been full of nothing but twists and turns, disappointments and reverses. It seemed unfair.

Cheerlessly, he fixed his eyes on the far bank. Destiny's small face, riddled with fear, came between him and the rim rock on the opposite shore. What would become of the child if Paul Wickerton became her father? Abandonment? Abuse? Death?

Howard lowered his head into the darkness of his cupped hands. "God," he prayed, "I have failed You. I blamed You when Cassie left me and took my dreams with her. It wasn't Your fault. Perhaps You can use even my mistakes and failures for Your glory. Today I give my disappointments to You. They are too heavy for me to carry. Show me the way out of my bitterness, and help me to walk in newness of life. Teach me to trust You." He paused. "And please protect little Destiny from the likes of Paul Wickerton. Amen."

Drowsiness, precipitated by the warmth of the day and the gurgle of the stream, closed his eyelids. Peace he hadn't known for many months engulfed him. Even the brook seemed to cease its threshing to burble along in a gentle song of tranquillity.

Then a voice, shrill with artificial gaiety, awoke him. "Howard! What a lovely hideaway you have found! May I join you?" Roxie was beside him, much too intrusive. "I've been wanting to visit with you, to become better acquainted. What finer time or place than this? Isn't it primitive, though? At least it is a respite from that dreadful inn! You must be as bored here as I am."

"Actually, I—"

"I know," she put words in his mouth, words that he had no intention of saying, "you will leave for the city as soon as you get your mother delivered from that sniveling moll. Wasn't it unfortunate that Dorchan fell and injured herself? *If* she injured herself. I think it was all a grand farce. But surely it won't be long until we can be on our way.

"I'm sure you know that the only reason I am here is on Paul's account. He is madly in love with Dorchan, and the only way he could come was on my finances. My father left me quite wealthy, and I couldn't bear to see Paul, a cousin of mine, pining away for his sweetheart." Roxie could prevaricate as easily as she could breathe.

"Why Paul insists on marrying a girl so lacking in proper conduct I cannot imagine. Heaven knows I've tried to talk him out of it. But he is stubborn headed, bent on digging his own grave.

"The only bright thread of this whole trip was knowing that I might see you again. I knew you would be lonesome for some life and a friend like me in this forsaken place. Isn't there a town nearby where we could find some entertainment? The inn is *dead*. Mr. Randleman would have twice the business if he would put in a bar and some gaming."

"Thank you, but I'm finding these moments relaxing."

"Oh, certainly. For variety this trickle of water is pleasing, but you and I can't be satisfied here for long. When do you plan to return to Kansas City?"

"I hadn't planned—"

"Oh, but listen, Howard. I found you a marvelous position there. They will take you on my recommendation. You can be president of a large company in no time flat. And the money flows! I was thinking that we might travel back together. As soon as Dorchan is well enough for the trip, Paul plans to take her back to Chicago, and you can worry no more."

"Chicago?"

"Paul's mother, my Aunt Mary, lives near there. That's where Paul and Dorchan will be married. Mary has everything ready."

"I'm not sure . . . that Miss Brown will marry Mr. Wickerton."

"Oh, I'm certain she will. She's just a bit offended right now. There was a misunderstanding, really. She thought there was another girl, and she ran away in a jealous fit."

"I heard her child, Destiny, say that Dorchan had someone else in mind."

Roxie gave a sawed-off laugh. "She instructed the child to say that to get even with Paul. Lovers' games are so ridiculous! You can't believe what a child says anyhow. The infant is only three or four years old. How should she know?"

"She is intelligent beyond her years. Anyway, for the child's sake, I hope that Miss Brown doesn't marry Mr. Wickerton. He will not make a good father."

The laugh turned raucous. "You are right on that score, Howard. My cousin has no patience with little people. He considers Destiny a nuisance. But Paul's mother, Mary, is quite fond of the little girl, and she will shield her from Paul's tyranny. Paul knows which side his bread is buttered on. You needn't worry about the kid. She has Mary wrapped around her finger."

"But she needs a father who loves her."

"Dorchan should have thought of that four years ago."

"I consider it noble of Dorchan to rear the child for someone else."

"Noble?" Roxie rolled her eyes. "There's nothing noble about Dorchan Brown. If she had any sense, she would latch onto my cousin to cover her shame. Don't let her pious face fool you, Howard. I've been sent by your guardian angel to rescue you!"

She inched closer, grasping his arm. A sudden reminiscence seized Howard, a vision of Kona. He was back in the captain's quarters of a Mississippi River boat. The door was bolted, and he was smothering. . . .

With an abrupt movement, he jerked away from Roxie's possessive hand and flung himself into the stream, boots and all. He had to get away! This girl was as full of subtlety as Kona. After what she had told on Dorchan, what might she tell on him?

He crawled. He swam. He fought the current. Then on the other side, Howard pulled himself from the water, dripping wet, and disappeared into a clump of trees without looking back.

He circled around, crossed a wooden footbridge a half mile downstream before turning back toward home. Safe on his own turf, he parked his waterlogged boots beside the back door, intending to tiptoe to his bedroom for a change of clothes. His mother must not see him; she would ask why he was soaked, and he didn't wish to explain about Roxie. That would be one more thing for Elizabeth to fret about.

Once inside, he heard voices and halted. Dorchan and his mother were conversing in low tones but not low enough to shortchange his keen ears.

"Paul says he really loves me, Elizabeth," Dorchan said. "And he must since he came all the way to Texas searching for me. I suppose I am being unreasonable in refusing to marry him right away."

"Do you love Paul?"

"When I left Mary Wickerton's a few weeks ago, I thought I did. I had spent three years planning a lifetime with him. But now I am unsure. I know God brought me here. I am happier than I have ever been. God gave me a good job, loving friends, and a chance to have my own business. But Paul says I am being selfish."

"Marriage is a serious commitment that begs being sure," counseled Elizabeth. "Poor Emmett joined with Parmalea unadvisedly and has suffered ever since. 'Marry in haste, regret in leisure' is what my mother always said."

"But I really must come to a decision. It is not fair to keep Paul waiting. I am costing him time and money."

Howard clenched his fists until his fingernails bit into the palms of his hands. He wanted to scream. *No! The man holds no affection for your child. Only in your presence does he treat her well. Behind your back, he is unkind to her. Today he started to injure her. He has an evil heart. Don't marry him, Dorchan!*

But what Dorchan decided was none of his business. He was only here for a few days to get his bearings; then he would be gone again.

"I will pray with you about the matter, Dorchan. You are more like a daughter to me than a friend, and I want only the best for you."

Bless his mother! If anyone had a telegraph line straight to God's throne, it was she.

"Oh, thank you," Dorchan said. "I want to do the right thing for myself, as well as for my child."

SEVENTEEN

COERCION

The need for something to drink was driving Paul mad. It was high time that the matter of marrying Dorchan be swept up to a climax. With Howard Brinnegar hanging around, he needed to get Dorchan out of Elizabeth's house.

Once he got her to Illinois and the troth was pledged, she wouldn't leave him even when she learned of his fatal flaw. Recently, he had seen Dorchan on the porch, talking with Howard; they were standing too near to each other, and that kindled Paul's flash-fire temper.

He couldn't afford to let the cheese slip off the cracker through his own carelessness. What further coercion could he employ to win her? In an effort to add to his arsenal of ammunition, Paul cabled his mother. Would she send Dorchan a message, persuading her to return to Illinois? He would forgive all her mistakes, and she would be back in his good graces if she could help woo Dorchan back for him.

Mary, who had spent a lifetime humoring her son, wrote the letter beseeching Dorchan to marry Paul. She was homesick for Destiny, she soughed. She wanted Paul and Dorchan to take over the farm. Paul needed a help-meet, and who would be more suited than Dorchan, who, having lived there for three years, already knew the inner workings of the place? The proprietress of the dress shop said she would be delighted to buy Dorchan's handiwork again, and at a higher price.

Paul even sent Roxie to visit Dorchan, anticipating that Roxie would point out his better qualities. With Dorchan out of the way, he soliloquized to Roxie, she would have a better chance of winning Howard for herself. Howard might be carrying a torch for the pretty seamstress under his mother's roof, accounting for his cold-shouldered treatment of Roxie. "When Dorchan and I have gone, Roxie, Howard will be yours," Paul promised. "A pawn in your hands."

Roxie might even try to provoke Dorchan to envy, Paul suggested. She could mention a few other young women in the wings who would be glad to get a prize like Paul for a husband. "Use any tool in the shed," he urged. "Considering our past and the demons we befriend, each of us needs someone for balance, an influence toward God. If after marriage life gets tedious, we can always slip off to feed our vices, with our spouses none the wiser. We'll look after each other, you and I."

Thus Roxie called on Dorchan. "My dear Dorchan," she gushed, "how fortunate you are to hold the happiness of such a marvelous man in your hands! Why, think of all the girls Paul could choose, and he is simply crazy over you! He's astute. Good-looking. A college graduate. That man is going somewhere in life. And his mother loves you. Some people have all the luck! Oh, that I had your chance!"

"You can have Paul, Roxie—"

"Oh, no, no! I am not nearly as suited to Paul as you

are. I would be doing him a disfavor to pursue him. I know nothing about farm life, and he tells me that you are in your element in a rural setting. I, like Howard, belong in a city. I am absolutely stagnating here, but I promised Paul that I would stay until his wedding."

"I have some misgivings about marrying Paul."

"Please share them with me."

"I am not sure that he can adapt to fatherhood. He pays little heed to Destiny."

"He'll be a natural, Dorchan. All men are. Right now he has other things to think about; he has a lot on his mind. He is worried sick about you. Truly, I see nothing but a happily-ever-after for you and your daughter. Paul says his mother already considers the child her grand-daughter."

"Yes, Mary loves Destiny. We were in Mary's home for most of Destiny's life. It troubled Destiny to leave Mary, but Elizabeth has filled that vacancy. God doesn't shut one door without opening another."

"You must be forthright with yourself, Dorchan. You planned to marry Paul when you ran away. You made your wedding dress for him. Why are you hesitating now?"

"I guess I really can't answer that. But things have changed in the past few weeks. I have found fulfillment here. The Brinnegars are more like family than acquaintances. There is a special dimension to Elizabeth's care; there is no partiality with her. She treats me as well as she treats her own son. Then there is Emmett Randleman. He has been like a father to me, like a grandfather to Destiny. He has gone far beyond the call of duty to see that I have a chance to get established in life."

"But surely you want a companion, a husband."

"Yes, but that will come in its time."

"One must open the door for opportunity when it knocks. Paul has gone to considerable expense and time to find you. He traveled hundreds of miles when he could have taken a wife from the university. Why? Because he loves you. Fate led him to me so that I could bring him to Salado. It was no coincidence. Can't you see that? Opportunity knocks but once, you know."

"Mrs. Brinnegar and I are praying—"

"I see no reason to pray when the answer is right under your nose, Dorchan." Her words pressed and pushed. "Anyhow, God leaves some things up to us. It is rather audacious of you to ask God to make up your mind for you when He has more important things to do: keeping the stars from colliding, scheduling the seasons, giving angels their orders. . . .

"Paul cannot wait indefinitely. He has work to do back home. His stay here is expensive. He is making a great sacrifice and all for your benefit."

"Real love will wait. If Paul is impatient, he can go home."

"And return later? Would it be square to ask him to make another costly trip?"

"I could go to him."

"His purpose for coming was that you would not have to make the trip alone."

As Roxie pelted her with reason, Dorchan wilted, and her hands fell like lifeless objects into her lap. "Then I'll . . . I'll try not to keep him waiting much longer."

Still Roxie dug for deeper trenches. She had nothing concrete to report to the man who sent her, and that would not do. He would be angry. "You are strongly considering marrying Paul, aren't you?"

"Yes. It is probable that I will. I suppose I have no reason to disappoint him after he has come all the way to Texas for me. I . . . I just wish that I felt for him what I once did. . . ."

Roxie's voice softened. "It will come back, dear Dorchan. Paul tells me that there were many misunderstandings. He said that his mother told you—"

"His mother told me nothing. I happened to overhear a conversation between Paul and his mother, though I was not eavesdropping. He told Mary about a woman at the academy, a woman he planned to marry. It hurt deeply."

"Now you know, of course, that Paul never planned to marry another woman. He was being sarcastic. He told me about it."

"Yes, and that is all in the past. I must forgive Paul and forget it."

"That's the Christian way." It was Roxie's finest argument, and her smile showed that she was pleased with herself.

After Roxie left (and reported every syllable to Paul), Paul came again. Like the torrent that beat against the wise man's house in the biblical parable, gust after gust came to weaken Dorchan's resolve.

"My sweet Dorchan," he dissembled, "I have just come to realize that, unfortunately, you heard my rash remarks to my mother when I was in the throes of emotional prostration over my final examinations. None of what I said was true, of course. I was being caustic.

"I have loved you since the day we met. When you and that precious baby came to us, I said to myself, 'There's the girl of my dreams. When I finish my education, I will marry her if she will have me.' Believe me, there was never anyone else. I invented the girl and her name, Aurilla. There was no engagement and certainly no marriage!"

Dorchan looked directly into Paul's eyes. "In that same conversation, you questioned my morals."

"I was testing Mother. I wanted to force her to defend you, to trust you, to treat you as your purity deserves."

"And Paul, I want a husband who will love my daughter." Her gaze held.

"Now, Dorchan, you cannot expect me to have the same feelings for the child as you do. She has been with you since she was a small infant, and I have only seen her on the occasions when I came home from school. And on most of those visits, my mother had so mollycoddled her that I had no chance for a real acquaintance. After we are married, we will work together as a family: me, you, and the child. We will work out our differences in an adult, rational manner."

It sounded good, but Dorchan didn't capitulate easily. The debate went on. "You wanted me to leave. You said so."

"It was a reaction to stress, dear. Have you never been to the breaking point? Have you never said anything absurd? I wasn't myself that day." He reached for her hand, but she withdrew it. "Look, Dorchan. Don't you think you owe something to me and my mother for taking you in and providing for you?" Paul talked too fast, tried too hard to be convincing. He attempted to impose his decision upon Dorchan as if she had no mind of her own. Instead of tearing down the wall between them, he only added more bricks. "We can repay Mother by taking over the farm so she will not have to work so hard in her old age."

"I owe you nothing. I paid my own way and more," defended Dorchan. "Without the room and board I paid, your mother could not have kept you in college."

"But Dorchan, who taught you your trade?"

Dorchan stood, bringing the argument to an end. "I won't be pressured into a wedding, Paul. We have a lifetime ahead of us. I don't see that a few more days could possibly matter that much. Love—if it is love—will have patience. I received your mother's letter, and I appreciate the invitation to return to Illinois. I know that you need a wife. I may be the woman you need, and I may not."

"You are most certainly the woman I need. Moreover, you are the woman I want. I won't settle for second best. And you need me, Dorchan, a man who can handle your affairs so that you won't have to worry about finances."

"I don't worry about finances, Paul. God has always supplied my needs."

Low intensity wasn't working. Perhaps harshness would be better. Sometimes a woman had to be taken in hand and told what to do, Paul thought; there came a time when a man had to assert his authority. "Come along, Dorchan," Paul's dictatorial voice bought space in the palaver. "You are being unreasonable about this. I want to be married immediately. We are going to the courthouse to get the legal part of this thing behind us today. After the ceremony is over, I will help you get packed for the trip. I shall wait no longer!"

The demand did not faze Dorchan. "I will tell you as I told Roxie. Elizabeth and I are making this a matter of prayer. I've told God that I want a principled man, a man with lofty motives, a Christian."

"Darling! I will never interfere with your religious beliefs or your church attendance! Please understand that. Now let's go." The yeast of frustrated waiting worked in Paul. He took her arm, but she slid away from his grasp.

"No, Paul. When—if we marry, I want a pleasant service conducted by a minister, my dress pressed, and a small reception at the inn orchestrated by Betta. I'm in no frame of mind for a wedding today. No real gentleman would insist. God will guide me to a proper decision. I know you are in a hurry to return to the farm, but I need a bit more time for reflection."

"Then you will return with me?"

"If God's answer is yes, I will."

On his way out, Paul vented his frustrations on the fence with a vicious kick. Destiny, playing nearby, fled to the house.

"Where have you been, Destiny?" Dorchan asked.

The child let out a tired breath. "Just making winding roads in the dirt. All my roads are winding.

"Mommy, why did that man stay so long? It's hot outside, and I am tired."

"You could have come in."

"No, I couldn't." A frown of irritation badgered the little face. "Why does he come every day?"

"He wants to be our daddy."

"But he is the one who didn't want us, remember? And he doesn't like me. He would never pick pretty flowers with me or go fishing or play Hully-Gully. Besides, he kicks things. Mommy, *please*, don't get him for our daddy. Get Mr. Howard. He's nice."

EIGHTEEN

THE PHOTOGRAPH

It rained during the night. Dorchan liked the clean, washed feeling as if the whole earth had a bath. She breathed deeply into the thickness of humidity, filling her lungs with the early morning freshness.

Leaving Destiny asleep, she took Helga's dresses, finished to the last detail, to the inn, where she would meet her customer. Displayed on wooden hangers, Helga's wardrobe hung in a neat row. It had been an gratifying commission; Dorchan had done her finest work. There was a russet foulard printed with tiny flowers, an ocher silk, a cobalt blue in satin, and a green muslin printed with roses. Helga would go back to Pennsylvania well clad.

Betta, knowing that Dorchan was coming, made apple tarts, oozing delicious juice and capped with fine, snowy sugar. "Howard picked the apples from the orchard last evening and brought them to me," she said. "That Howard is a fine specimen of manhood. I'll be sorry to see him go. I wish he would stay on."

Dorchan didn't want to hear about Howard's leaving. Her mind balked at the idea. "Has the inn been quiet lately?" she asked, steering the talk away from a subject that brought unaccountable angst.

"Mornings are always peaceful," outlined Betta. "That Roxie girl sleeps until noon. But at night! Sometimes she and her friend talk until the wee hours of the morning. And in her room! Why, no decent girl has a gentleman in her room ever. She's of this shameless modern stock, though. Spirits know their own kind when they meet." She cut her eyes from side to side and then went on in a hushed voice. "I'll be glad when that one is gone. She has a prissy mouth, and she is trouble. But then, Parmalea likes her."

"She will likely leave when Paul Wickerton does."

"I expect so. She is paying for his room, too."

"She is?"

Betta gave a shudder. "That man makes my skin goosey. Those eyes of his shift around. My maw used to say, 'The tongue may lie, but the eyes never.'"

"Is he here?"

"No, ma'am. He got himself up and left this morning before breakfast, and I'm gladsome. He hied off earlier than usual. I sometimes wonder what he is up to."

So Betta didn't know that Paul was in Salado to propose marriage to Dorchan. Fine and well. Dorchan didn't want her to know. "Will you help me pray about something, Betta?" she asked abruptly.

"My prayer bones are for sharing, Dorchan."

"I am trying to make a decision whether to stay in Texas or to move back to . . . to Mary's house in Illinois. It is a very important matter. Mary wrote and asked me to come back, but I want to do God's will."

"God says He will lead in a *plain* path. Never doubt God will show you His will plainly, because you are His child. I don't want you to go away, but we'll pray and see what the good Lord says."

"Thank you, Betta. Elizabeth is praying, too."

Helga came, ending further discussion between Dorchan and Betta, and Betta returned to the kitchen. The easterner crowed with delight over her garments. "I'll be obliged to come back every year for more new clothes," she vouchsafed. "I trust you will be here next year, won't you, Miss Brown?"

"I'm . . . I'm not sure. I . . . I may move back to my former home. That is, if I decide to get married."

"Oh, my lovely seamstress! As much as I would miss you and your talent, I do hope that you find marital bliss. There is nothing more wonderful than a loving companion. I was lost when my husband went on to heaven. There is not a day that I don't relive the precious memories of our time together. If you've found your soul mate, you shall never regret the union, Miss Brown. But when will this wedding be?"

"In a week or so."

"Will it be here at the inn?"

"Likely so."

"Ah, I regret that I can't stay over to meet the lucky groom, but I have already overstayed my original plans. Aren't these southerners hospitable, though? Such courtesy makes me wish that I might move to Texas.

"However, I have obligations in Pennsylvania. Besides my own property to keep up, I have my deceased sister's place to oversee. I rent it out, and it nets a fair profit. But it makes me ever so uncomfortable to collect the rent money, for I know it doesn't belong to me. I use a portion of it on repairs, but the rest is in an account doing no one any good. What should I do with it? My husband left me sufficiently fixed. I have no children, and I really don't need the income from my sister's property."

"Perhaps you could give it to a good cause. What was your sister's favorite charity?"

"I don't really know. She was quite religious."

"Did she like children?"

"Oh, she loved children! She wanted scads of them."

"Maybe you could donate the money to a home for orphaned children."

"Oh, yes! That would be grand!"

"I was reared in an orphanage. Our rooms were cold, our covers ragged, and our food in short supply—mostly coarse, dark bread. I can think of no greater need."

"You lived in an orphanage?"

"All of my childhood was spent in a poorhouse for children."

"Did your parents die in the plague?"

"I know nothing about my parents."

"You poor, poor dear. I wish that I could have known. My husband and I would have been glad to adopt you."

"That would have been lovely. But I probably wasn't eligible for adoption. The man who dropped me off there promised to return for me. He never did. And, too, if I had been with you, I wouldn't have been in Chicago to get my little daughter when the great fire came."

"Your daughter?"

"Destiny. She is the joy of my life! Her mother died in the fire, and I have had her since she was newly born. Sometimes I forget that she isn't my own."

"Then that's another reason for you to marry, isn't it? So the child may have a loving father figure and grand-parents. Children need complete families if their minds and emotions are to be whole. But there, who would real-ize that more than you?"

"Wouldn't you think a stepfather must be a special man, wisely chosen and sanctioned of God?"

"Indeed! A mother must not think only of herself but of her child as well. But I am sure that you have chosen that special man, Miss Brown. You are certainly an excep-tional young lady, worthy of the very best."

Helga reached into her handbag for the money to pay Dorchan for her work. "You have done such an exemplary job—and have been a comrade yet—that I would like to pay you extra, dear." She handed Dorchan forty dollars in crisp tens.

"Oh, no! No!" objected Dorchan. "That is far too much!"

Helga shook her head. "A wedding gift," she said, "for a dear, dear friend, one whom I shall never forget. May your future be filled with sunshine."

A wedding gift. Is this a sign from God that I should marry Paul? The question came of its own voli-tion, but Dorchan was forced to shelve it to answer Helga's next question. "Miss Brown, what will your new address be? I want to keep in touch."

"Just write to me here," Dorchan instructed. "Dorchan Brown, in care of Salado Inn. Mr. Randleman will see that my mail is forwarded."

"Dorchan? Is that your first name?"

"It is an unusual name, isn't it?"

"Did the orphanage give it to you?"

"No. The man who left me at the shelter also left a handbag. In the bag was a photograph of me with that name written on the back."

"I've only heard that name once before. That was the name of Velma's baby. Dorchan Fay Webbster. I remember asking Velma where on earth she came up with that name for a girl. Oh, and I have a picture with me of my Dorchan."

Helga hung the clothes on the hall's cloak rack and rummaged in her purse, removing a small picture. "Dorchan was her auntie's greatest joy! I grieve for her yet."

When she handed the photograph to Dorchan, Dorchan caught her breath and made a thin sound, half sobbing, half laughing. The room blurred out of focus with the veil of tears, taking the picture with it. It was a photo of the same child in the same setting as her own. Dorchan turned the print over, and on the back in the same script were the words: *Dorchan at six months*.

Helga Harper was her aunt! She threw her arms around Helga and clung to her.

NINETEEN

Rescue

"You will come with me!" Paul dragged Destiny along toward the Brinnegar home place, his lips locked in a cruel line. The child struggled to escape the bruising grip of the hand that held her.

"Turn me loose!" she cried.

Paul's only response was a mocking laugh.

"You're hurting my arm."

"You are going with me to tell your mother that you want me for your daddy."

"But I don't want you for my daddy."

"Listen, you little devil. I will cut off your ears if you don't say what I tell you to say. Then if you tattle, a bear will eat you alive."

They had almost reached the porch when Howard Brinnegar sallied forth from a hedgerow. "Take your hands off the child, Paul Wickerton."

"This is no business of yours, Brinnegar. I am making a call on my espoused, and you will not interfere. Oh, I know that you want Dorchan for yourself, but she doesn't want you, a jobless, uneducated nobody. She wants me." Flames of hostility blazed in Paul's eyes, beetling his brows.

"This has nothing to do with Dorchan. I said, let the

child go." Howard's tone implied there would be conse-quences if the man didn't obey. "You are causing her pain."

In response, Paul gave the child's arm a savage yank, and Howard landed a crippling blow on his flaccid biceps, frogging the muscle. When Paul jerked back to retaliate, sputtering curses, Destiny slipped away and ran.

"I am warning you, Paul. You are never again to come on this property and lay a hand on the child, or you'll wish you hadn't." Howard turned to stride away but turned back. "Anyway, Dorchan isn't home."

"How do you know so much about Dorchan?"

"I happened to be the one who took her to the inn this morning in my mother's buggy."

Howard could have said nothing that infuriated Paul more. Wrath showed in every movement of his body, his rigid walk, the slinging of his head. Watching until the man left, Howard went back to the garden.

Just before noon, Elizabeth called for Destiny to come in for a snack. Destiny didn't answer. She called again. And again. Then she went in search of the child. But Destiny was nowhere to be found.

"Howard," she said, "have you seen Destiny?"

"I saw her about an hour ago," he said, offering no further information.

"Where was she?"

"In the front yard."

"I can't find her anywhere. Please help me search for her."

A jagged fear ripped through Howard's heart. Had Paul Wickerton come back for the child? Howard's long legs made a quick circle around the house, but the child was not there. Elizabeth worried aloud, "She never leaves the yard. I can't imagine her just walking off."

The front gate stood ajar. "I think Mr. Wickerton frightened Destiny this morning, Mother. He was pinching her arm, hauling her toward the porch when I stopped him."

"I didn't know that Paul Wickerton had been here today."

Howard's look was cold. "Unfortunately, he has."

"You don't suppose he . . . took Destiny?"

"I hope not. I should think he would hesitate to touch her after the threat I dished up for him."

"Oh, Howard! You're not causing trouble, are you?"

"No, ma'am. But I will not stand by and see a child injured by a ruffian. Paul Wickerton is the one causing trouble."

"If Destiny was disturbed, she may have tried to go to the inn to find her mother. I will walk toward the inn, and you walk toward the river."

Howard headed down the trail that wound its way to the creek, calling as he went. Before long, he picked up the child's footprints on the rain-softened earth, and a terrifying possibility clenched his heart. What if the child had made her way to the river and fallen in?

The indentations made by Destiny's feet took little detours into the woods where the tops of flowers were missing. Destiny had gathered a bouquet of wildflowers as she went along. For her mother, no doubt. With a child's intuition, she must have sensed the struggle that her mother was experiencing. She was too young to understand, too old to be unaware. And she would want to be of comfort.

Dorchan was a good mother, a brave woman. Howard refused to believe that she had betrayed her virtue. He believed her pure, true to herself and to God. Certainly, she was too noble for the likes of Paul Wickerton, a man with a deformed soul in whose nature rode greed, idleness, and discourtesy. He would like to tell Dorchan so, but what right had he?

He was hardly a paragon of perfection himself, but he had always treated children kindly. Even in his prodigal days, he hadn't used God's name in vain or touched a drop of liquor. And he had brought himself back to his heavenly Father, unworthy of sonship but willing to be a servant.

He had suffered, but so had Dorchan. She'd had more than her share of heartaches, and she, a woman, had handled life's knocks better than he. And now, what if something happened to the child for whom she existed? Howard groaned, but the sound issued more from his heart than from his lips.

He sped down the narrow path, running now, chased by panic. No sound reached his ears save the gurgle of the water; no small voice responded to his calling.

At water's edge, the footprints disappeared. Fear slithered in his stomach. She was gone! She had fallen in, had been swept downstream, and had drowned. Howard felt his cheeks wet with tears.

No, Lord. Please. Not this. What will Dorchan do? Paul Wickerton would not be deeply grieved at the loss of the child. He might, in fact, be relieved. Oh, he would pretend to be distraught, but his distress would be a subterfuge all on the surface, all to impress Dorchan. He cared naught for the little girl, and he had occasioned her death by his rough treatment this morning. Scared, Destiny had run away to hide from him. Dorchan would never know the real reason for the child's uncharacteristic action.

Howard slung off his boots and plunged into the current. The day was damp, making the spring-fed water seem colder. Looking to his right and then to his left, his vision only settled for tiny moments of concentration then moved on. He scanned the stream from bank to bank, up and down. Nothing.

He would have to tell her mother. He'd have to tell Elizabeth. He'd have to tell Emmett and Betta and Puddin. He'd have to tell them that the golden-haired angel who brought such brightness to their lives had taken wings. Remorse twisted inside of him, swelling in a fresh gush of tears to distort his sight. How could one find words to tell the unspeakable?

But wait! What was that speck of color against the brown log downstream? He waded toward it, keeping a precarious balance in the pushing stream.

And there he found her. At first he thought that her lifeless body had been snagged by the fallen tree, but as he drew nearer, he realized that she clung, shivering and alive, to a branch. When he reached her, she tried to smile, but her blue lips could only manage a quiver.

"Destiny!" he rejoiced, his relief as exaggerated as his earlier anxiety. "You hung on until I got here!"

"And I prayed," she said, teeth chattering. "I'm c-c-cold."

He lifted her gently and saw that her arms were scratched and bleeding. Ripping off his own shirt, he wrapped it about her. "We will get you home and into some dry clothes."

"My foot hurts," she fretted. "A rock rolled, and my foot turned upside down. That's why I fell into the water."

"You've sprained your ankle."

"I was hiding from *him*. Please don't let him hurt me and Mommy, Mr. Howard. You are good and kind, but he is not a good man. He is mean."

"He is no man at all, Destiny. Real men never hurt women and children. I won't let him hurt you. And that's a promise." He emphasized the last word.

"But Granny Elizabeth said you were going away soon. The man will be glad, and he can hurt me when you are gone—"

She was small. She was defenseless. And she knew it. Howard could not ignore her plea for protection; he could not abandon her for his own selfish pursuits. He would postpone his plans for her sake. "I will stay a while longer."

Back at the house, Howard turned Destiny over to Elizabeth and went to the inn for Dorchan. Dorchan had said that she would walk home, but some call on Howard's heart sent him for her. He would tell her about Destiny's mishap, but he would keep his opinions to himself. Destiny could tell her mother why she had left the yard.

TWENTY

BUSINESS TRIP

Word of Dorchan's windfall spread from mouth to mouth, hastened by the adroit tongue of Betta, who could keep neither good news nor bad. The hearsay mushroomed as it went. Dorchan had been discovered by a blood relative, the whispers relayed, and was heiress to a vast estate.

By the time the story reached Paul Wickerton, Dorchan was proclaimed heir presumptive to half the state of Pennsylvania, indubitably rich. She had money. She had property. She had prestige.

He licked his chops at the conjecture of a cushy life with no work and plenty of cash for booze. How lucky could a fellow get? He *had* to win her now!

That bit of news called for celebration with spirits. He had shunned the bottle as long as he could. The times he'd slipped off for small nips didn't suffice; he needed a real bender. Lately, his craving for the brew had made small irritations twice their size and hard to tolerate. His forbearance was skimpy, and he had almost bungled his ambitions when he roughed up Dorchan's child. A trip to the saloon would put him back on track, make him less edgy. Now that the financial rewards would be well worth the extra time and effort it cost him to succeed, he would need to have his wits about him. Calm and collected—that is what he would be after his spree.

To this end, Paul left a note for Dorchan that he needed to go to town on "business." He would be gone for two or three days, he wrote, and he hoped that she would not miss him too dreadfully. He would be ready to start for Illinois when he returned if that was agreeable with her. They would have the nuptials here with her friends, or they would go home to Mary, whichever she preferred. He would bring "his little daughter" a surprise.

It would work! He could afford to cotton to the kid, buy her a stick of candy. Children forgot all grievances when presented with sweets; children hadn't a memory. And he would bring Dorchan a nice gift. Roxie would advance him the money for these indulgences.

During Paul's absence, Helga sent Dorchan an invitation to spend a day with her before she boarded the northbound train for Pennsylvania. The day and place she chose was Bell County's annual Labor Day picnic in the park at Belton. The festive affair, complete with games, contests, and the best of southern cookery, spawned reunions from miles around. *Now that we've found each other,* Helga penned, *we can have our own reunion!*

I'll come for you, Helga wrote as a postscript.

It will be out of your way to come for me, Dorchan wrote back. *I'm sure Elizabeth's son won't mind to drive me in to Belton. I will meet you there.*

Destiny's foot was still swollen, but she was improving. With a child's ability to snap back and three days to go, she would recuperate in time for the reunion. Now that she had reached the "restless" stage of recovery—too active to be confined and too confined to be active—

Destiny demanded both Dorchan's and Elizabeth's attention. "You're wearing us out, Destiny," reproved Dorchan.

"But my mind wants something to do, Mommy," the
child whimpered. "I wish I had my books from my trunk
in our room at the inn."

"I'll send Howard for the trunk," Elizabeth spoke up.

Howard heard. "And whose slave is Howard
Brinnegar?" He winked at Destiny.

"Mine!" she cheered.

"Just because I went fishing and caught a little girl
instead of a perch!"

"And when I'm well, we'll both go fishing and catch
that perch!" Destiny's eyes danced.

"As you say, madam." Howard bowed so low that he
almost fell headlong into the floor, bringing a peal of giggles from Destiny.

Destiny liked Howard, and she disliked Paul. Howard
hadn't tried to establish an affinity with the child; it had
happened naturally. Why couldn't Destiny interact with
Paul like this? What was amiss? Why must all her life be
such a puzzle?

Heart sore, Dorchan trudged upstairs to finish a dress
she had started for the day in the park, a day of revelation
destined to change her life forever.

TWENTY-ONE

REVELATION

Dorchan read stories to Destiny until the child fell asleep, but she read by rote. Her mind was elsewhere, scourged by a thong of unrest.

With plenty of daylight left, she sought a citadel where she could think. Much had changed in the last week. She had discovered who she was. She had a birth date: September 25, 1852. She had a legal name: Dorchan Fay Webbster. And she had an aunt: Helga Harper.

God had saved Destiny from drowning though it was yet unclear to her why the child had wandered off to the river in the first place. Destiny had been warned about leaving the boundaries of the yard, and she was not a disobedient child. Howard, wonderful Howard, had found her, and Dorchan owed Elizabeth's son a great debt of gratitude for saving her child's life.

To compound her mental upheaval, she had promised Paul an answer to his marriage proposal. He was away on a business trip and would want to leave for Illinois when he returned. And she was no closer to a decision now than she had been when he showed up in Salado a month ago. Why were answers so difficult for her? And where could she go to think? To pray?

The church. A place of solitude. A place of meditation.

It was but a mile away, and she would be back before dark. The double-rutted road that led there was winding, reminding her of Destiny's fascination with crooked roads. The child especially loved this one.

An urgency gripped Dorchan with such forcefulness that she found herself running. Her spirit was running. Her emotions were running. Were they running toward Paul or from him? How could she know the difference?

As the church came into sight, Dorchan slowed; she didn't wish to go panting and puffing into God's sanctuary. He would want her to come serenely and peacefully into His house. And with utmost trust.

However, before she approached the church's front door, she saw someone kneeling in the cemetery. It was a man, and he embraced a monument. *Howard!* What was he doing here? She heard his wracking sobs as he laid his head against the headstone.

She suspected that he had come to mourn for his father. How he must have loved the man! So moved was Dorchan by Howard's grief that she was beside him before she had time to rationalize her action. "Mr. Howard," she whispered, "can I help you?"

Then she read the inscription on the stone: *Katrina Brinnegar, beloved wife.* And beside it, a small grave bore a carved monument: *Newborn Brinnegar, Heaven's lamb.*

Reality screamed at Dorchan, and she sank to her knees beside Howard. Pulling a handkerchief from her pocket, she wiped away his tears and then stanched her own. "I . . . I didn't know," she sympathized. Howard's young wife and baby were buried here.

Red-rimmed eyes met Dorchan's, eyes that held an

agony of thought. "I blamed God for taking her. Then I blamed everything on the baby's birth. If Cassie had been stronger . . . I lost them both in one day."

"I'm sorry."

"I have kicked myself over and over because I wasn't home when they died. If I had just known what would happen, when it would happen . . . At least, Katrina's mother was with her. . . .

"But it is time to let the guilt go. It is time to let Katrina and the baby go. I can't hold them any longer. They belong to God now. I . . . I had to come today to tell them good-bye. I had never let myself say it. It seemed too final. I thought that time would blunt the spike of memory, but it hasn't. I must do it myself. None of us can live on water that has gone downstream."

Dumplings of clouds formed in the west, shadowing the sinking sun. "It must be hard for you to come here to church every Lord's Day," Dorchan pitied.

"Yes, it has been hard. I didn't want to come back to Salado at all. This is where we grew up together, Katrina and I. This is where we courted, where we married. We pledged our vows in this church. But God sent me back to teach me that we cannot run from the ghosts of our yesterdays.

"I went to St. Louis to get away. There I turned my back on God. But I had a praying mother. Her prayers followed me. I hadn't planned to return at all, but . . . but I thought there was a problem here that concerned my mother, so I came to iron things out.

"I didn't mean to stay this long, and I think that I shall be moving on soon. But I had to make peace with myself, with my past. God gave me the courage to make this step

167

today—it was a hard one—and I am trusting that He will show me the path for tomorrow."

"I . . . I will pray for you."

"Cassie (that's what I called Katrina) was Emmett and Laura Randleman's only daughter."

"Emmett Randleman is your father-in-law?"

"Yes. He has suffered, too. He lost both his daughter and his grandchild. His wife's memorial is here in this cemetery, too. Death is no stranger to my father-in-law. Sometimes I think an unfortunate marriage is worse than death, though. Emmett married a woman who did not understand the grieving process. Parmalea despises the mention of Cassie or the baby. She is jealous of Emmett's former life, his happy memories."

"Oh, Howard!" Unconsciously, Dorchan had left off the "mister."

"I vowed that I would never love anyone else, Dorchan. My trust was gone. What if it happened a second time? What if I lost again?"

"You lost your child, but you saved mine. I haven't had a chance to thank you. I would like to do that now." She kissed his cheek and fled into the evening that fell in streaks of red and yellow paint.

TWENTY-TWO

THE NOTE

It was a day that Emmett Randleman would never forget, a day earmarked for tragedy. Had he known what its full and ironic conclusion betokened, he would have wished to stop time, to eradicate it entirely from life's calendar.

The inn was full as was usual for the Labor Day weekend. Since last evening, Emmett had been turning people away. He found it necessary to make an early morning run to Garden City for supplies; Betta was out of coffee and sugar, and the flour bin was below the level of safety.

On an ordinary day, Emmett would have commissioned Howard to go for the needed stock, but Howard had asked off to take Dorchan and Destiny to the Belton festivities, where they would meet Helga Harper. Emmett had a few hopes battered of late that he would not admit to. One was a hope that Howard might become interested in Dorchan. But it had not happened; Howard had spurned all romantic involvement since Katrina and the baby died, and there seemed no chance for a resurrection of such feelings. Second, Emmett had adopted Dorchan and Destiny in his heart to replace his own losses, and the revelation of a living kinswoman to claim them disappointed him.

Now, Emmett wished more than ever that his son-in-law would find an attraction to Dorchan. That would anchor her and Destiny to him, to Salado. Until now Emmett had considered Howard smart to sidestep a second marriage since his own had proved disastrous. But Dorchan wasn't like Parmalea. Dorchan was not a demanding person; she would make Howard a gracious and loving wife.

Emmett had tried his best to make Parmalea happy, but he sorely missed Laura. And somehow he had not been able to keep his loneliness from showing. Laura had been a domestic goddess who loved to please her husband and her daughter. She made quilts and jellies and wrote poetry for the ones she cherished. A woman such as she was hard to forget, yet Emmett had never thrown her proficiency up to Parmalea. That would be both unfair and unkind.

Parmalea was the sort, though, that couldn't put a matter to rest. She probed and dug and made rude remarks about Laura and Katrina to keep the wound fresh. She was not willing to let the sore places heal over, allow the bleeding to stop. Emmett had even ceased attending church to please her. She accused him of looking out the window toward the cemetery while the service was in progress. Any visits he made to the churchyard must be done in secret.

With the overflow crowds at the hotel, Emmett supposed he had not given Parmalea enough attention lately. To make restitution, he bought her a box of candy at the drugstore. She loved chocolate. He tried to crowd out thoughts of Laura's response to the smallest of gifts. "Oh, my Emmett!" she would exclaim, bright-eyed, "you are earth's most beloved husband! What did I ever do to deserve you?" If Parmalea bothered to thank him for the candy, it would be with a sneer or, "Why don't you do this more often, Emmett Randleman? I dare say you brought Laura a bigger box than this every day!"

Shadows shrank toward their noon positions, prodding Emmett to hurry the supplies to Betta. When he arrived at the inn, the cook brought him an envelope that bore his name. She had discovered it on a table when she went to clear away the breakfast dishes.

Dusty and hot from his trip, Emmett sat down with a glass of lemonade to catch his breath. He pulled out the note, and Betta heard his glass clatter to the table. She ran to his side. "What is it, Mr. Emmett?" The man's hand shook as if it were palsied. "Is it bad news?"

He shoved the lavender-scented page toward her. *Emmett*, it said, *I am leaving with my dearest friend, Roxie Rail. I can bear the boredom of this place no longer. Surely you know that I do not love you and never did. We walk along different strata in mind and in spirit. Roxie has offered to set me up with a lucrative job in her field. I have accepted her offer and feel an immense release. I am happy, and eventually you will be happy, too.*

As a last endeavor to dispatch my responsibility at the inn, I have given Paul Wickerton Dorchan's room since they will be wed immediately anyhow. That will free up another room for paying guests.

You are bound to know that I am not your type, Emmett. You have turned religious, and you should marry someone like pious Widow Brinnegar. You two would make a good match with your "holier than thou" attitudes. I have given you a miserable life, but

I make no apologies as you have done the same for me. I hope that you will enjoy your freedom as much as I plan to enjoy mine.

The note was signed by Parmalea in her handwriting with no endearments. When Emmett and Betta went to Parmalea's room, it was empty, swept, and ungarnished.

"Well, blow ole Betta down!" ejaculated the cook. "She took everything but the spittoon!"

"Did I mistreat her, Betta?" There was pitiful resignation in Emmett's voice.

"Mistreat her? Now look here, Mr. Emmett!" blurted Betta, her remarks stripped of lace. "She hounded and chased you something scandalous. She had the finest clothes money could buy, plenty of food and servants. She didn't turn a tap if she didn't want to. She nagged and fretted and bellyached. Not once did you strike her or demean her or even give her the words due her ears. Many a time I saw you return good for her evil. Your wife was a dissatisfied woman, Mr. Emmett, and if she had stayed here a thousand years, you couldn't have pleased her. You and the inn are better off without her. So there!"

"I will not divorce her, Betta. She can come back anytime she wishes."

"That is more than generous of you, sir. And when that two-faced Roxie girl deserts her, she will be slinking home with some of that pride lopped off!"

"If she comes back, Betta, give her a charitable welcome."

"If you say so, Mr. Emmett. And don't worry over the inn. I will see that the business is not upset by the going of the mistress."

"I'll raise your wages."

"No, you won't. I'm not worth a penny more than I'm getting, and I won't accept another dime."

"What did Parmalea mean by moving Paul Wickerton's belongings into Dorchan's room? Dorchan hasn't mentioned a wedding to me. Oh, I do remember that Mr. Wickerton laid some claim to her the night she stumbled and fell, but she denied it. And I suspected all along that she plans to stay with Elizabeth until the man takes his leave. It seemed to me that she wanted no part of him."

"I don't know what Parmalea meant. But I know that Dorchan wouldn't want a man's toiletry in her room. And I shouldn't think she'd marry that skunk if she did marry. He ain't worth a bullet. Shall I check Dorchan's room to see if Mr. Wickerton's belongings are there?"

"Yes, and if they are, set them out in the hall. I will ask him to pay for his own room or to move on." He pushed back his chair. "I have some accounts to work on for the next hour or so. If you need me, I'm in the office."

Betta, unceremoniously tossing Paul's boots and hat from Dorchan's room, heard the proprietor call. She dropped Paul's valise and took herself to his office.

"The money is gone, Betta. All my savings. Every cent of it. Only Parmalea knew where I kept the key to the safe."

"I'm sorry, Mr. Emmett. The woman is lower than I thought."

"I did not dream that my own wife would steal from me!" Emmett's face twisted. "If she needed anything, she had but to ask, and it would have been hers."

"Well, we can be glad that you just bought supplies, and the inn will not be without necessities."

But it wasn't the end of the day. The worst was yet to come.

TWENTY-THREE

A DAY IN THE PARK

An east wind tempered the heat. Howard waited for Dorchan and Destiny to ready themselves for the trip to the park. "They've trapped a fine day for a picnic," he commented to his mother. "I'll probably stay a while myself." He invited her to go along, but she begged to be excused.

"I have a few things I want to get done today," Elizabeth said. "The pears cry for canning, and I promised to help Puddin grind up the green tomatoes for the chow-chow. Puddin says we should get ready for winter."

"September has just begun, Mother!" countered Howard.

"I know, I know, son. But you know Puddin. She thinks ahead. We want to make extra preserves this year so that we can share with Emmett at the inn. Parmalea refuses to can anything, and Emmett gets ever so hungry for homemade marmalade like Laura used to make."

"Parmalea won't like it if you make preserves for Emmett."

"Then she can get off her lazybones and learn to do something herself."

The statement was so out of character for Elizabeth

that Howard laughed aloud. When it came to Emmett Randleman, she was defensive. Howard supposed that if his father had died before his father-in-law remarried, his father-in-law might have become his stepfather. Emmett and Elizabeth had always been dear friends, congenial and helpful neighbors. After a fashion, they took care of each other. Had Emmett been a man who dwelt on might-have-beens, he probably would have given a few wistful thoughts to the wifely qualities of Elizabeth Brinnegar, but he wasn't that sort of man.

How his father-in-law could abide Parmalea's dark temperament, Howard did not know. She wasn't anything like Cassie's dear, self-sacrificing mother. Emmett, in his lifetime, had been called upon to live under two extremes as far apart, considered Howard, as heaven and hell.

Dorchan came downstairs, a warm glow visiting her cheeks. Holding Destiny's hand, she was clad in a new dress that accentuated the amber highlights of her hair. "We're ready," she announced.

"You are taking a bonnet for Destiny, aren't you?" Howard reminded. "We don't want our little Destiny to get sunburned."

Our little Destiny? The single phrase—with all it might mean, with all it might not mean—sent Dorchan's heart into a spiral inside her chest. Since Howard had rescued her daughter, he seemed to claim part ownership in the child. He had bonded to her. And that was not good. What would he do when she married Paul or moved to Pennsylvania or—?

"I have her bonnet in my handbag."

The road to Belton was lined with vehicles. People swarmed from every direction in hacks, by horseback, and on foot. "Are there always this many people?" Dorchan asked.

"I haven't been to the celebration in four years," Howard said. "The crowd has grown considerably since Cassie and I came."

It is good for Howard to talk so casually about his wife, Dorchan thought. *The healing has begun.*

Dorchan had little problem finding Helga. Her aunt had claimed a thickly foliated tree as her territory in Babel and had spread a blanket under the leafy canopy. She motioned for Dorchan to join her. "Just look at that!" she pointed toward a fifty-foot plank table the men had constructed. "We're in for a feast."

As more campers arrived, the tables sagged under the strain of their culinary arts. Potato salad. Sauerkraut with sausage. Cottage cheese. Cakes and pies and rolls and cobblers. Kettles of beans and sides of beef, barbecued. Coffee pots simmered on open fires, diffusing a rich aroma. Smells and sounds meshed together to create a potpourri of delightful fellowship, fostering a festive atmosphere.

Howard offered to take Destiny to watch the contests while Dorchan and Helga visited. He was hardly out of sight before the two women lost themselves in a world of catching up.

"Oh, my Dorchan, my niece! I can't believe we found each other!" prated Helga. "If Velma could know! Now, you know, don't you, that I want you to make your home in Pennsylvania near me? It's colder there in the winter, and the people are more formal. But you will be with me much of the time, and I will treat you like a daughter."

"That sounds marvelous, Aunt Helga," Dorchan said,

177

"and I would like that. But you will remember that I have a suitor, and he is wanting us to get married right away."

"In my elation, I had forgotten about your engagement. Now I remember your mentioning it to me. But, of course, he will come to Pennsylvania, too."

"I'm not exactly engaged. That is, I haven't said yes yet."

"I should like to meet this young man," jibed Helga, "to see whether or not *I* will say yes."

"You shall meet him if he returns before you must go home. He left a few days ago on a business trip."

"If I can persuade you to accompany me to Pennsylvania, I will postpone my home going once again."

"Finding you has added a new dimension to my life, Aunt Helga, and has given me something else to pray about. It may not be the proper time for me to wed. Perhaps the Lord would want me to go back east with you, at least for a few months."

"It is rumored that distance makes the heart grow fonder."

"And rumor makes the heart grow distant," laughed Dorchan. "Now tell me all about myself. From the beginning. What were my parents like?"

"You are a combination of both," profiled Helga. "However, you bear your father's favor more than mine or Velma's. But you have Velma's personality. You walk like her, talk like her, laugh like her. Isn't it strange how heredity works?"

"You and my mother were identical twins?"

"No. Our hair, eyes, and coloring were the same, but Velma was shorter, more padded than I, and much prettier. I was the skinny, freckled-faced one. Velma also had the more winsome ways. The young men tripped over their feet for her attention; she could have had any one of the boys in our school class. But she wanted none of them.

"She had her heart set on Jacob, a widower who lived in our neighborhood. Velma loved God, and so did Jacob. They saw eye to eye on the Bible.

"Jacob was ten years Velma's senior. She was eighteen when she married him, he twenty-eight. Our mother thought the union a mistake, but as it turned out, Jacob adored Velma. They were blissfully happy. Jacob had a home near our own, and when we found out that you were anticipated, we threw a party.

"Jacob was one proud papa when you were born. He called you his star. You were a contented baby who belonged to all of us.

"Then Jacob got word that his brother had struck gold in California. Talk of the gold find at Sutter's Mill had been going for two or three years, and Jacob thought it foolish to work for a pittance in Pennsylvania when he could go west and make a fortune.

"I begged Velma not to go with Jacob, but she wouldn't be left behind. They were inseparable. Velma had just turned twenty when they left with you, their six-month-old baby.

"Before they left, I had your picture taken, thinking, *Dorchan will be walking and talking when I see her again.*"

"Well, I am!" Dorchan interjected. "But go on."

"Jacob and Velma only planned to be gone for a year. I sent a few things along with Velma: a writing tablet, a parasol—"

"I had the parasol! It was destroyed in the fire."

"And I made you a little brown cape."

"I had it on when I was turned over to the orphanage. That's how I got my name: Brown."

"Well, when that wagon pulled out, I cried and cried. I had nothing but a broken heart and a picture of my little niece.

"I got two letters from Jacob. In the first, he said Velma had taken a fever. In the second, he told me that she had died but that he was going on to California. He would be back as soon as he'd made his fortune. He made no mention of you in the letters.

"Then we were notified that the wagon train had been robbed somewhere in the badlands of Nevada and that all the occupants had been murdered. I supposed you were killed along with your father."

"Do you suppose it was my father who left me at the orphanage?"

"I think so."

"Why?"

"After losing Velma, he didn't want to lose you, too. He was aware of the dangers of the trip. He probably figured he could make it, a grown man, but he couldn't risk the life of his baby. He loved you too dearly. He planned to come back for you."

"Yes, he told the home that he would return and would bear all the expenses of my care. I'm sure he didn't know what an orphanage was like."

"He didn't. Jacob had no experience with such places. No doubt he thought that would be the best and safest place for you. However, had he let me know that you were alive and where you were, I would have gone for you.

That's the mistake he made, not letting someone know."

"God had a plan of His own."

"I never knew where Jacob buried Velma. Men are so brief in their posting. I cried myself sick."

"And then you lost your husband?"

"Yes. He was injured in that terrible war between the North and the South. He fought for what he thought was right; I was proud of him. He caught lead in his leg, and the wound never really healed. He lived a year, but he wasn't well the whole time. Poisoning set in, and the doctors took the infected leg. But he was too weak to recover. That left me with no one. You are my only living relative. All that I have will be yours when I am gone.

"And now let me tell you about your property. You have a large home in a good location; property has appreciated tenfold in the last twenty years. You could sell your place and be fixed for life. Also, the rent money has been accruing interest. I haven't touched any of it except to make needed repairs. I'd like very much for you to come to Pennsylvania."

"I wish I knew what to do, Aunt Helga. Five months ago, Paul Wickerton was the man of my dreams. I had my wedding dress ready—"

"Tell me something about this admirer."

"He finished his schooling this year. He is highly educated, and he has a lovely mother. His father is deceased, and his mother wants us to take over the farm in Illinois. His looks serve him well, but . . ."

"But what? There should be no 'buts.'"

"I don't know. I can't seem to get a 'go ahead' feeling in here." Dorchan touched her chest. "Oh, there were some petty problems, a few misunderstandings common to any courting couple, but nothing important. I thought he had someone else at school, and he didn't. In my confusion, I packed up and ran. I should have stayed put."

"No, you shouldn't have!" contradicted Helga. "Then we never would have met."

"Now, in a different setting, I can't seem to recapture my first love."

"The man who brought you here today, the man who has Destiny, he is just a friend?"

"Howard is a fine man. He has been married, and he lost a wife in childbirth. He has built a wall against further hurts. He isn't interested in remarriage."

"That's a shame. He would make someone a good husband."

Suddenly, Dorchan stiffened and grabbed Helga's hand. "Auntie! Here comes Paul Wickerton, the man who has asked for my hand in marriage! I . . . I thought he was away on a business trip."

"Then I shall meet him."

From the look on Paul's face as he approached, it wasn't going to be a pleasant meeting for any of them.

TWENTY-FOUR

LIES

Paul, compliant to Roxie's plot, had returned to the inn for the two women. The three of them, he, Roxie and Parmalea, made their getaway along with Emmett Randleman's money while the inn's proprietor was in Garden City buying supplies. Betta, in the kitchen setting her salt-rising bread, didn't hear the trio's exodus.

Emmett had almost caught them. Amid the jostle of wagons, the bubbling froth of people going to the picnic, he had not recognized his wife hidden behind an umbrella. But she had seen him. Paul, recuperating from a four-day drinking binge, was scarcely sober when he picked up his passengers.

"Did anybody see Dorchan while I was gone?" he asked the women.

"Oh, yes, Paul," babbled Roxie. "She's been to the inn broadcasting her wealth. And there's news."

"News? Does it concern me?"

"I would say that it does."

"If it has anything to do with Howard Brinnegar—!" His eyes turned to flint.

"It doesn't. Dorchan has decided to go home with the rich relative from back east."

"Without me, she won't go anywhere."

His eyes bright with grandiose plans to spend Dorchan's bounty, Paul strutted about the park as if he owned the grass and trees. He flirted and winked at the girls without a hint that Dorchan sat in the shade of a majestic oak, talking with her newly discovered aunt.

Paul's gait was rather unsteady, and the town's marshal stopped him. "Son, have you been drinking?"

"No, sir!" thundered Paul. "I have a crippling disease known as St. Vitus's Dance, and I have just taken my medicine. My mother and my sister are here in the park somewhere, and they can verify my statement."

"No problem, son. It is my responsibility to make sure. Also, sir, we're searching for a young woman by the name of Roseanne Altruso. She has been described to us as having very black hair and dark brown eyes. She is of medium height and weight and is around twenty years of age. There is a warrant out for her arrest. You seem to be getting around a bit. Have you met anyone by that name and description?"

"I haven't, but I'll be glad to help you look for her. Why is she wanted?"

"Grand larceny."

"Is there a reward for her capture?"

"There is."

The marshal went his way, and Paul happened upon Roxie and Parmalea, sauntering their way toward the river. "Hey, girls! We're in for some fun," he announced. "The law is looking for a girl out here. Her name is Roseanne Altruso, and there is a fat reward for finding her. Medium build. Black hair. Twenty or so. Let's join in the egg hunt."

Roxie didn't blink. Her face might have been etched

in stone, so inscrutable was her expression. But she did tuck her black hair under her oversized hat. "I'll help," she volunteered. "Come on, Parmalea. This is more fun than the games. Where is that officer, Paul?"

He pointed toward the long table, and Roxie went to search for him. "Sir," she said when she found him, "I understand that you are looking for a Miss Roseanne Altruso."

"Do you know her whereabouts?"

"I don't know where she is now, but she stayed at Salado Inn last evening. I talked with her. Oh, she was a wily thing, all right! Right away, I said to myself, 'That young woman is trying to hide something!' Being a friendly lass, I tried to make friends with her, but she was guarded, close mouthed. And she toted this *big* purse. It was big enough to swallow a bank vault! She never laid the purse down anywhere even when she ate. Doesn't that seem odd? And such black hair you never saw! Black as an iron skillet. Long and silky—"

"Might she still be at the inn?"

"No, she left for Austin by stagecoach first thing this morning. I fear she has given you the slip. Had I known she was wanted, I probably could have detained her."

"Thank you for the information, Miss—"

"Rail. R-a-i-l."

"Have a good day, Miss Rail."

Paul hurried to them, his unsteady walk slowing his pace. "And do we get a reward for the tip, sir?" he asked.

"Not until the criminal is found."

The officer was joined by another. "We have a clue, Buck. This is the best lead we've had all day."

A bystander started the fun. "Let's give the lady who

185

tipped the lawman a penny!" Considering it part of the day's sport, the crowd rained pennies at Paul's feet, and he snatched at them eagerly.

But Roseanne Altruso didn't pick up one. She had Emmett Randleman's savings at her disposal, and that is all she and Parmalea would need. For after today they would be leaving the country. And one thing was sure; they wouldn't be going toward Austin.

TWENTY-FIVE

THE ANSWER

Malicious distrust possessed Paul Wickerton when he met with Howard Brinnegar. For Howard had Dorchan's child by the hand, and it appeared they were having a splendid time at the Labor Day picnic.

Here was the child he had but lately planned to woo with candy. It looked as though another man was trying to outmaneuver him; Destiny had a lemon drop in her sticky fist. If the old saying "The way to a mother's heart is through her child" was true, then Howard must have ulterior motives in showing the child about. He had heard about Dorchan's money, and he wanted it!

Well, he would not have it. Paul would snatch the child from him, buy her something better than a lemon drop and return her to her mother, who was probably right now sitting at the sewing machine at Elizabeth's house. Likely, Dorchan didn't even know where her daughter was. It was akin to kidnapping, taking a child without her mother's permission. One could get in trouble for that, and Paul would like nothing better than to get Howard Brinnegar in trouble. In fact, he'd be delighted to land the man in jail. Thereby, Howard would be out of the way.

"I like the races that must wind around to get to the

end; don't you, Mr. Howard?" Destiny looked up into Howard's face.

Howard patted her hand. "Yes, I do. We're having a good time, aren't we?"

Bah! Paul thought. Howard wasn't having a good time. He was licking the calf to get the cow! He needed to be taught a thing or two. "What do you think you are doing with Dorchan's child?" barked Paul, and Destiny jumped in fright.

"Why, we're enjoying God's beautiful world, Mr. Wickerton," answered Howard, pleasantly enough. "With so lovely an escort, I find this a special day indeed."

"Naturally you would. But let me remind you that the little girl doesn't belong to you, and you have no right to take her so far from her mother without Dorchan's permission."

"Our stroll is with her mother's permission, to be sure, Mr. Wickerton."

"I shall see that she gets back to her mother at once." Paul lurched for Destiny, but his foot caught on a malignant root. He sprawled across the ground, a comical sight. Howard hurried to help him regain his footing.

"Don't lay your vile hands on me!" demanded Paul. "You are a snake in the grass. I know you are a sneaking thief. You are trying to steal my woman! And you'll not get her. Do you hear?" Bitter derision curled his lips. He struggled to rise, and then he pushed his face so close to Howard's that he announced by his breath he had passed some time in a taproom.

"You've been drinking!" Howard said.

"I have not. And if I had, what is it to you?"

"It is against the law to be intoxicated in a public place."

"I am not intoxicated. I am angry. Indignation and intoxication are poles apart. I want you to return the child to Dorchan. *Now.* Dorchan would not want her child seven miles away."

"Seven miles away? Destiny is within fifty yards of her mother. Dorchan is sitting on a quilt under that oak tree, talking to Helga Harper, her aunt." He pointed toward the women, cloistered in conversation.

Paul shambled in that direction, the look on his face determined.

Dorchan and Helga stared at him. "What are you doing here, Dorchan?" he blustered.

"Oh, Paul, I am glad you have come. I want to introduce you to my Aunt Helga from Pennsylvania. We have but recently found each other, and we can't get enough of learning of each other's lives. Helga and my mother, Velma, were twins. My mother died on a trip to California, and Aunt Helga assumed that I had died also. She had a picture of me in her purse, and when she showed it to me, I recognized myself. You see, I had a picture just like hers. Isn't it unbelievable? We decided to come here to spend a great day together."

Helga extended her hand. "Hello, Paul."

Reaching for Helga's hand, Paul pitched forward, scarcely avoiding a fall.

"Are you ill, Paul?" Dorchan asked. "Your eyes are dreadfully bloodshot. Maybe you should sit here in the shade for a while."

"No sleep," excused Paul. "Hours of business."

"Dorchan tells me that you are a college graduate. What business are you pursuing, Paul?" asked Helga.

"Uh . . . er . . . trying to buy a team of horses to take

back home with me," he supplied. "You have to stay awake all night and watch horse traders. Dishonest, they are."

"Did you find a team?"

"Yes. That is, no, not yet. I'm trying out a set of bays today. My mother likes bays. She—that is—we need them on the farm." He hiccupped. "What I came to say, Dorchan, is that I think you should keep the little girl with you. I don't trust Howard Brinnegar. He might try to kidnap her."

It maddened Paul further when Dorchan treated the warning as a joke. "It's more likely that Destiny would kidnap Howard," she chuckled.

"I am serious, Dorchan."

"You have no worries, Paul. Howard would no more harm Destiny than he would his own mother! He is good with children. If he ever marries and has a family of his own, he will make a model father."

Her endorsement of Howard hit Paul the wrong way. When Paul drank, he had no self-control. He fought to keep his tongue manageable, but he had consumed too much alcohol. "I know what Howard is trying to do, Dorchan, even if you are a blockhead! He is trying to take you away from me one inch at a time. He knew you would be here today, and that's why he came. He thinks he is God's gift to women. But let me tell you, he is a nobody! And he's going nowhere. He thinks he is too good for Roxie, but he isn't good enough. He has no education. Look at me; I've been to college."

His words were wandering off the right track, but he couldn't seem to stop them. "Howard has heard that you have come into money. It's money that he wants. Your money. But he won't get it. If I can't have it, nobody will have it! I have ways of—"

"Please leave, Paul," Dorchan spoke quietly but firmly. "You have been drinking."

"I have not been drinking. I don't drink. And another thing," he was revealing things he hadn't meant to, "I don't appreciate my mother writing to you and blabbing about my first marriage. That was none of her business. If I wanted it told, I'd tell it myself. Aurilla wasn't worth the title of a wife anyhow. It's you I wanted to marry instead of Aurilla, and it's you I still want to marry. And it's you I will marry. I'll show Aurilla!"

"I will not marry you, Paul. Now or ever. I have been praying for an answer, and God has just given me one. With Aunt Helga as my witness, I vow that your chances of winning my hand in marriage are forever gone. Please leave."

In a wide emotional swing, Paul began to cry like a baby, and his voice slipped into a plaintive minor key. "I'm not drinking, Dorchan. You must believe me. . . ." The pitiful whine was followed by a wrathful roll of swear words.

Roxie came for Paul and led him away. It was the last glimpse Dorchan had of the man she once thought she loved.

TWENTY-SIX

THE DECISION

Roxie hurried Paul and Parmalea to the wagon. In a careless moment, she had let her cascade of black hair escape from her hat, and several people had gaped at her. Or so she imagined. She thought she heard one whisper, "That must be Roseanne Altruso. . . ."

"Let's get out of here, Paul," she urged, her voice tinctured with a hint of foreboding. "With my black hair, someone might get the mistaken notion that I am Roseanne Altruso. Then we would be in a pickle trying to prove I'm not."

Paul pulled a bottle from beneath the wagon seat and took a long draw. Things had not gone well for him, either. "Yes, let's go," he agreed. "Our zodiac isn't favoring us today. The posse is watching me, too. Everybody thinks I am drunk."

"You are."

"I'm not. Which way shall we go?"

"North. Toward Waco."

Paul whipped the horses into a frantic pace, drinking more as he went along the road.

"Slow down, Paul," cautioned Roxie after a few breathtaking curves. "You're going to roll the wheels off this crate, and I'm getting sick."

"Can't shlow down, shweetheart." His words were becoming thick and slurred. "Shee. They're after ush." He whipsawed from side to side on the driver's bench.

"Then let me drive. You'll get us killed."

"No! Let me drive. I'm shober enough—"

He may have made it had he not met with a blind corner. In his futile effort to get the vehicle turned, Parmalea was thrown from the wagon and suffered a broken neck.

"Paul! Look what you have done! Now we will be charged with murder!" cried a frightened Roxie. "And, oh, Parmalea was my friend! She was going to work with me in the dance halls. And now you've gone and killed her." Roxie broke into a fit of sobbing.

"Don't you cry, shweet Roxie," comforted Paul, giving her a slobbery kiss. "Ush will go back to Illinoish, and my mama will shee that we are taken care of. I will marry you sho you won't have to dansh. We'll be sho happy ever after. Let Howard Brinnegar have that shtuffy old Dorshan. He'sh not good enough for my shweet Roxie." Paul broke into an impromptu concert of ridiculous singing: "Oh, my darlin', oh, my darlin', oh, my darlin' Roxie shweet, . . ."

"But, Paul, I'm not sweet. I'm . . . I'm really Roseanne Altruso, and the Rangers are looking for me to put me in prison. I stole a lot of money—"

"And I'm shoushed, and they're looking for me to put me in the shlammer, too." He roared, a high, sodden laugh. "Doesh not matter what you've done, Roshie; they will never find ush. We make a perfect match, and they're no match for us."

"What will we do with Parmalea's body, Paul?"

"Shpread her out in this here road. Shomebody'll shee

her. Maybe the angels or the devils will take her shome-place."

"I'll take the money out of her purse, but I'll leave the identification."

"An' lesh be long gone, shweetheart."

The western sky flamed gold and rose when the next load of wayfarers came that direction and found the lifeless body of Emmett Randleman's wife. They took her to the undertaker, who notified her husband of the tragedy. He wept unashamedly.

"I had hoped that she would come to her senses and return to us," he told Betta, and his statement was undergirded with sincerity. "I hoped that she might learn to love me. Now I will have four graves in the churchyard to mourn."

A simple ceremony it was, with the preacher stammering a eulogy. He tried to find an encouraging word to say. Few had hopes of a restful hereafter for a woman who had no place for God in her life. Elizabeth lingered by Emmett at the grave, offering the comfort of a friend.

Parmalea's handbag was returned to Emmett, but the missing cash had vanished. Several folks were reasonably sure they knew who took the inn's savings and said so, but being the man that he was, Emmett refused to make an accusation.

Neither Paul nor Roxie returned to the inn; no one expected they would. Their names were dropped. Those who had known them tried to forget them.

Now one decision had been marked from Dorchan's list, but others remained. Would she move back to the inn and pursue her career as a seamstress, or would she travel to Pennsylvania and make her home under the roof where she was born? Many wondered, but nobody asked.

"Dorchan," Emmett broached, "I don't wish to influence you one way or the other, but it will be lonesome here without that slip of a girl. I'll be obliged to make Destiny's 'winding roads' in the sandbox by myself when she is gone. And it will look mighty peculiar for an old man to play in a sandbox."

"I don't know what God wants me to do yet, Mr. Randleman. I'm afraid I'm not very good at getting answers from heaven's postbox. God has to hit me in the head with a brickbat to make me understand what He is trying to say! A part of me wants to stay here, and a part of me wants to go with Aunt Helga. I know what is here—and I love all of you—and I don't know what awaits me in Pennsylvania. But I am willing to do whatever God chooses for me."

That Sunday, Emmett was at church. Elizabeth invited him to sit with Howard and her. They made a lovely family as natural as if they had sat together every Sunday of their lives. Dorchan took the bench behind them, but Howard kept glancing back. Dorchan supposed his attention strayed from the sermon to Destiny.

Just before dismissal, a beam of light pierced the window and fell across Dorchan's face. It flooded the dark places of her mind, and instantly, all was clear. Helga would be leaving in two days, and Dorchan would go with her.

Back to her beginnings.

To start anew.

TWENTY-SEVEN

ROAD'S END

Wishing to be alone, Howard went to the woods for a rendezvous with his Master. So disturbed was he that he had forfeited breakfast for a talk with God. All peace had fled his soul.

He was sure now that he loved Dorchan, loved her as deeply as his mending heart would allow. She was a beautiful woman inside and out. She would walk tall beside him as Cassie had done.

This morning he recalled everything incident to Dorchan: her graceful poise, her long hair dull gold in the shadows, her wide-set eyes with their dark lashes swept to copper-hued tips, her voice and how it thrilled him. . . . And that kiss of gratitude in the graveyard! It had stirred some forgotten desire within him.

While a brutal struggle warred in his breast, a quiver of regret passed over him that he could not marry her. He must be fair. Fair to her. Fair to himself. But mostly, he must be fair to the child. Destiny was not his flesh and blood. He could love her easily enough, but it would always be a bittersweet affection, a haunting memory, a wishing that the tiny form he had once held in his arms could have stayed on earth to bring him a father's joy. Each time he had taken Destiny for a walk, told her a story, or triumphed with her in a new discovery, the thought of his own child was there, pricking him, gouging him, diluting his happiness.

Howard didn't want to go on year after year to life's end with that nagging hurt. If that one pain could be removed . . .

Dorchan was at the inn packing at this moment. Packing to move to Pennsylvania. It made sense for her to go with her aunt, to go to her property. Why should she stay in a small hotel room and sew until her fingers ached when she could live in comfort in her own spacious home? Neither she nor the child had ties here. She had made the proper decision.

Certainly, there would be a husband for her someday if she wished to marry, a man who had never wed. A man who hadn't the mental embroilments of a widower who couldn't hold a child without pining for his own who had slipped away. A man who hadn't a tiny monument in a church cemetery to scream for his attention every Sunday.

Thankfully, Dorchan hadn't married that pernicious drunkard! After that day in the park, he, Howard Brinnegar, would have stepped in with some advice of his own had worse come to worst. Destiny wouldn't have a father like that one as long as Howard Brinnegar had any say.

Howard knew that his mother dreaded the parting. The incongruity of the past three months came back to amuse Howard. He had hastened to Salado to warn Elizabeth about an interloper who had latched onto her generosity, and he'd found one of earth's loveliest creatures instead. He had planned to stay two days, at the most three, and those days had stretched into profitable weeks. He'd found his way back to the Cross.

Howard also knew that Emmett dreaded Dorchan's going. With no grandchildren of their own, he and Elizabeth had opened their susceptible hearts to Destiny, too willing to avail themselves of a child's innocent love. Destiny had served as a substitute grandchild for each of them. Their lives would suffer a vacancy that nothing could fill.

As Howard started back toward the house, his heaviness deepened. Before his prayer, he had decided to speak with Dorchan. Since his prayer, he had made the decision to let her go. He would regret it, of course. He knew that he would. He had known that her leaving would bring pain since he first looked into her lovely eyes, since he carried her in his arms when she fell at the inn. But it was for the best. His best. Her best. Destiny's best. Joy and sorrow folded into one fabric, and he prayed that he would be man enough to accept it.

As he neared the gate, his mother waved frantically from the door. What had happened now? He tasted fear. His body urged his feet to a run. "What is it, Mother?"

Elizabeth stood, pale and shaken, tears raining down her cheeks. "Howard! Oh, Howard!" She buried her face in her trembling hands.

His heart leaped to his throat as he took both of her hands into his own in an effort to calm her. "Please tell me, Mother. Is Dorchan all right? Is Destiny all right?"

"Yes, son. They are all right. It's . . . I . . ."

"Are you sick or injured?"

"Only in my heart."

"Shall I send for the doctor?"

"No."

"Where do you hurt? Tell me quickly."

"It isn't a physical pain, Howard. Oh, how shall I tell you without hurting you, too?"

"Never mind the hurt to me, Mother. Just speak!"

The story came out in broken pieces. "I was packing the books in Destiny's trunk. Dorchan said to put them in the bottom. I took everything out, and on the bottom, I found—" she walked to the chair and picked up Destiny's baby quilt, the one she was wrapped in when Dorchan caught her, "—this. It is the quilt I made for Cassie's baby. I know it is the same one, for I embroidered my own initials in one corner so small that it would take an eyeglass to read them. She was so proud of it. Oh, what is the answer to this awful riddle? And why must the memories of my grandbaby be so painful?" She sank into a chair.

Howard was quiet, beset by a sudden melancholy. "I . . . I remember the quilt. It was Cassie's favorite."

A noise at the door abbreviated the conversation. "Be easy with the screen, Destiny," Dorchan was cautioning. "There, that's a good girl." Then she directed her attention to someone else. "Why don't you come in, Mr. Randleman? Elizabeth won't mind if you visit with Destiny for a few minutes."

Emmett, who had escorted them home, stepped through the door with Dorchan and Destiny. Once inside, Dorchan's gaze traveled from the frozen Elizabeth to Howard, whose jaw was taut and his face white. "Is something . . . wrong?" she stammered, embarrassed for both herself and the coach house proprietor. "Are we interrupting—?"

"The quilt—" Elizabeth held it up as if the showing of

it would solve everything.

"It is Destiny's baby quilt," Dorchan said. "I'm saving it as a keepsake for her."

"Where . . . where did you get it?"

"It was wrapped around Destiny when I got her."

"Exactly when . . . where did you get her, Dorchan?" Howard pried.

"I don't always tell the details of my getting Destiny because the how doesn't seem anyone's business, but since you asked—"

"Yes, please," urged Elizabeth, her hand on her throat. "Tell us."

"As I was fleeing the Great Chicago Fire on October 8, 1871, running for my life down Wabash Avenue, I heard a woman's voice from a balcony. When I looked up, a young mother with desperation in her eyes pleaded with me to take her baby."

"Could it be, Howard?" Elizabeth jumped up, bursting into tears. "Look! She has your eyes."

Howard caught his breath. "Wait, Mother. Let's hear the rest of the story."

"The mother dropped the baby into my arms and then disappeared into the burning building. The baby, a very tiny thing, was wrapped in that quilt. I have kept it for Destiny; it is the only thing she has left of her mother."

Emmett Randleman sat down hurriedly as if his legs would no longer support him. "Cassie went back into the fire for Laura," he said. "Laura was there, and Cassie would not abandon her."

Dorchan gave him a quizzical look.

"Dorchan," Howard continued where Emmett left off, his throat choked, "that was my baby you caught. Cassie and I lived in an upper apartment on Wabash Avenue."

"I made this quilt with my own hands," Elizabeth wept. "See? Here are my initials in the corner. I sent the quilt by Laura Randleman when she went to Chicago for the birth."

"My wife, Laura, died in the fire, too," Emmett's whole body shook with a tremor. "She went to Chicago to be with Cassie when the baby was born. She planned to come home on Tuesday, the tenth. But the fire came . . . and . . . and she didn't make it."

"Our baby was eight days old," Howard blotted away a stream of tears. "I worked for the city of Chicago, and they had sent me to Washington for some documents. I left on Friday before the fire broke out on Sunday. When I got back . . . everything was gone. . . . We had a memorial service and put headstones in the cemetery here, although there were no actual caskets."

"What was her name?" Dorchan asked, her question barely audible.

"We hadn't named her. We had agreed to do that when I returned from the business trip and before my mother-in-law left."

Howard saw the blood drain from Dorchan's face as she faced the moment of truth. He was Destiny's legal father; the child belonged to him. Dorchan was preparing to give up her rights to the child, and it was tearing her apart.

"Destiny," Dorchan licked dry lips, "you've always wanted a daddy. Howard is your real daddy."

"He is?" Destiny pirouetted in a childish jig. "Oh, goody, goody! He's a nice daddy. He will pick flowers with me and go fishing and play Hully-Gully." She ran to

Howard to be smothered in his arms.

"My little girl!" Howard's voice broke. "Oh, my precious daughter!" The tide of emotion was as unutterably sweet as the blaze of sunlight to one long in darkness.

"My granddaughter!" beamed Elizabeth.

"*My* granddaughter!" added Emmett.

Destiny pulled away with a perplexed look. "But you'll still be my mother, won't you, Mommy?"

Pain cramped Dorchan's face. She opened her mouth to explain to Destiny, but Howard intercepted. "With all my heart, I love my daughter. But I love you, too, Dorchan. Will you be Destiny's mother?"

"Will you be my mother, Mommy?" Destiny mimicked.

"Will you be my daughter-in-law, Dorchan?" Elizabeth teased.

"Will you be *my* daughter-in-law?" chimed in Emmett.

Elizabeth set her arms akimbo. "Your daughter-in-law? Emmett Randleman, are you proposing to me?"

"Well, not exactly," grinned the man, "but I will if you'd like."

"I'd like. We can tie this family up in so many knots that naught can pull it asunder."

"Yep. My son-in-law's wife will be your daughter-in-law and my daughter-in-law-in-law."

"Now you've lost me, Emmett Randleman," Elizabeth said.

"No, I've just found you, Elizabeth. In this tangle, nobody could get lost, ever."

"It seems you might as well start unpacking, Dorchan," Elizabeth resolved, looking ready to help. "We'll get Helga to move to Texas. There's too many of us to move to Pennsylvania."

"Wait!" Howard waved for attention. "Dorchan hasn't given her answer yet."

All eyes turned upon Dorchan, waiting. "What woman ever had four proposals in one day?" Her eyes twinkled. "The answers are yes, yes, yes and yes!"

Howard still held Destiny as if he dared not let her go lest this be only a fantasy that could slip away easily. He shook his head to clear the cobwebs. "Her name fits. Destiny. We could write a book. *Destiny's Winding Road.*"

"I like winding roads," Destiny reminded.

"I do, too," Howard set his daughter beside him and reached for Dorchan with eager arms, "when they dead-end like this."

About the Author

LAJOYCE MARTIN, a minister's wife, has written for Word Aflame Publications for many years with numerous stories and books in print. She is in much demand for speaking at seminars, banquets, and camps. Her writings have touched people young and old alike all over the world.